MEMORY

SKYE MALONE

Memory
Book Seven of the Awakened Fate Series

Published by Wildflower Isle | PO Box 129, Savoy, IL 61874
www.wildflowerisle.com

Cover design by Karri Klawiter
www.artbykarri.com

ISBN-10: 1-940617-58-8
ISBN-13: 978-1-940617-58-9

Library of Congress Control Number: 2016906808

Join Skye Malone's mailing list to hear about new releases!
www.skyemalone.com/mailinglist

PRONUNCIATION GUIDE

Dehaian (deh-HYE-an)
Greliaran (greh-lee-AR-an)
Ruanir (ru-ahn-eer)
Strakirin (strah-KEE-rehn)
Yvaria (ih-VAR-ee-uh)

LOGAN

Smoke and flames poured from the wreckage of the warehouse, blackening the midmorning sky. Red, white, and blue lights spun madly atop emergency vehicles all around.

It looked like a celebration of America in the middle of hell.

I kept my eyes on the rubble while I climbed from the back of the black sedan. The warehouse walls had caved inward, sagging toward the ground like a deflated child's toy. Steel girders remained like blackened bones, wavering in and out of sight behind the flames. Fire crews blasted water at the blaze, though even I could see their efforts were mostly designed to keep the flames from spreading. Nothing could be done to save the building.

But then, that had to be the idea. The Judiciary wouldn't want human authorities finding any trace of what was probably inside. Yet why Judge Engle had called me a few minutes ago, insisting I come to the site of this destruction, was anyone's guess.

I strode away from the sedan, straightening my designer

jacket while I went. I knew the driver would stay put. To a person, the servants of the Marseilles household were charity cases my mother acquired, destitute and desperate ruanir who'd screwed up their own lives in one way or another. The Judiciary was benevolent, though. More so, really, than I believed they needed to be. Mother and the other judges refused to leave those failures out in the cold. Instead, they gave them a place to live, to work, and a way to earn back the Judiciary's trust in their ability to live as a ruanir should. And as a result, those ruanir knew they owed us everything. They would never be so foolish as to move a muscle without permission.

By the rear of an ambulance, I caught sight of Judge Engle. Tall, black-haired, and dressed in a dark suit, the man appeared more like an old-world preacher than anything. The aura of frozen dignity and silent power that all members of the Judiciary possessed only added to the image. His back was to me, meaning I couldn't see where he was looking, but even the humans around him seemed to pick up on his energy. The EMTs moved like they were afraid they might say the wrong thing and be devoured by hellfire.

I buried a smile. What I had now was good: girls who fawned for my attention, guys who crawled over each other to be my friend, servants who were desperately afraid of offending me. Plenty of women had told me over the years that I looked like a model, and on top of that, I was the son of one of the highest-ranking members of the Judiciary. But what the judges had? Now *that* was power.

Someday soon, it'd be mine. Head of the Judiciary, most

feared judge of all time, that would be me. I never thought small, never bothered. I knew what I was capable of and what I could become. People called me *sociopath*, *psychopath*, and all manner of insults—or they did till I could arrange for something appropriately unfortunate to happen to them. But their words didn't matter. I knew the truth behind their pathetic fears.

No one in the world was like me.

"You called for me, sir?" I asked when I neared the vehicle.

Judge Engle turned. A large bandage was taped to his right temple and blood stained the white gauze. Dirt and soot smudged his face and hands.

It took less than a heartbeat to weigh potential reactions before I settled on the one that was most advantageous, the one that would elicit the best response from the judge in front of me. I blinked with shock. "Sir, a-are you okay?"

Judge Engle didn't respond. He glanced to the back of the ambulance, where the EMTs were working on some unconscious, blond-haired woman lying on a gurney, and then he motioned for me to follow him around the side of the vehicle.

I did. He drew a breath, seeming to consider his words. I waited. I was used to it. My mother spoke in exactly the same way. All the judges did. They didn't think like me, didn't have the same control of themselves as me—no one could have—but they came close.

"Your mother told you of our project?" He kept his voice barely above the engine rumble of the idling ambulance beside us.

I nodded, carefully hiding any reaction but polite obedience. I'd been annoyed as hell when my mother told me yesterday about the Judiciary's plan to capture the Beast and change Ariabella Moreau into something not-remotely ruanir. The idea of that ancient monster being back was disconcerting, sure, but Ari had been a hobby of mine for a while now; a little fallback for when I got bored. It wasn't that she liked me—far from it. But watching her seethe and squirm while her mother practically whored her out for my favor had been all *kinds* of entertaining.

But then, the Judiciary wouldn't care about that.

"Somewhat, sir," I replied. "It's the reason my mother asked me to fly out here last night. But I don't understand what I have to do with—"

"Training, Mister Marseilles."

I killed the rest of what I'd begun to say. "Of course, sir."

His attention flicked around the lot, as though making sure no one could overhear. "The creature escaped. Miss Moreau did as well."

I hesitated. I could act concerned, but that might seem weak. Alarm was better. "Oh my God." I looked to the building.

"Quite."

I glanced back, reading the tone and his lack of expression. There was something else. "So then…" I prompted. "The Judiciary has a plan, of course."

Judge Engle's lips thinned. My alarm wasn't feigned this time, though I didn't let him see it. They didn't have a plan? He and my mother had been put in charge of this project; how could they not have a contingency—

Wait.

I scanned the massive concrete lot surrounding the warehouse, finding the EMTs, the humans, the wounded enforcers and assorted ruanir nearby.

But that was it.

I looked back to Judge Engle. "My mother. She—"

"The Beast killed her."

I didn't move, didn't even blink, while the information sank in. The Beast. Killed my mother.

My mother was dead. This… this was…

Impossible.

Unthinkable.

And inconvenient as *hell*.

"The Judiciary requires your assistance," the judge continued.

My attention returned to him.

"Your position is being elevated, Mister Marseilles. The Judiciary is willing to lift you from novitiate status to provisionary journeyman for the purposes of this mission—and to maintain that status upon its successful completion."

Part of my mind filed the information away, while the rest still raced to process the implications of losing my mother, my advantage, one of the primary cruxes of my plans. Leveraging her authority was a key component of my ambition to eventually rule the Judiciary. Journeyman status would be useful, though. There weren't that many steps on the road to becoming a judge. By the time you reached the level of novitiate, the Judiciary already believed you had the potential to join their number. Journeyman was only one level below becoming one of them fully.

And nobody was promoted this young. I was nineteen. I hadn't even gone through the adjustment yet, when the magic I'd taken in over the years would finally slow down my aging. To reach journeyman status now would make history, considering it normally took till at least your late twenties, if not longer, which could translate into *decades* in human years.

"What would you have me do?" I asked.

"You know the girl, perhaps better than much of the Judiciary. You dated her briefly some time ago and you both have kept in contact since then."

I didn't contradict him, though that wasn't precisely true. I'd done her a favor and gone on a single date with her—she was attractive enough, after all, despite the fact she was basically a nobody. I'd started kissing her, and any moron could've seen that she wanted it, but the minute I began undressing her, she'd freaked. Acted like she hadn't understood the point of why I'd agreed to go out with her. And just as I'd started to get irritated, the panicky little bitch hit me with a burst of magic that had left my head ringing for days.

I was still working on a way to make her pay for that.

But meanwhile, her mother wanted me around. If I went for cougars, that desperate skank would've let me into her bed in a second, solely in the hope that I'd grant her access to the judges. Meanwhile, my own mother couldn't care less about the prude daughter of some failed Judiciary applicant or his conniving ex-wife.

At least, my mother *hadn't*.

Shivers crawled over my skin.

"We believe, if Miss Moreau were to see you, that she might not react as she would to an enforcer," Judge Engle continued, pulling me back from the path my thoughts had taken. "You may succeed in getting closer to her than otherwise would be possible, especially considering her current condition. Additionally, you could have insights into her behavior that could prove beneficial. Therefore, we would like you to lead a team of enforcers in a search for her—and the creature."

I was silent for a moment, evaluating this. "You want me to find the Beast?"

"It has taken human form."

I almost choked. It'd done what?

"The Beast can now appear as a blond-haired, muscular young man, approximately eighteen years of age." Judge Engle's mouth thinned again, the expression drawing his face into sharp lines. "The Yvarian king's lover resurrected the creature and has taken command of it. We believe its human appearance is an invention of hers, perhaps a device to better control the monster or assist in communication. But it has the unfortunate benefit of hiding the Beast from our sensors, rather like camouflage. It has been accompanying Miss Moreau in this form."

"So I need to get her away from that thing and then bring her back to you," I stated, wondering where he was going with this. Okay, so the Beast looked like a person. Great. It meant I knew who to be on the lookout for.

Judge Engle paused, his gaze tracking a fireman passing nearby. He waited till the man had gone. "Not precisely."

I let my confusion show.

"The Beast possesses the capacity to form empathic connections. We believe that this was how the ancient dehaians attempted to control the creature. But we used this for our own purposes and connected Miss Moreau to it. Thus, if it is too far from her, she and the creature will experience pain. If you try to steal her away secretly, the creature will know. Against all probability, the Beast seems to actually have formed an *emotional* connection to her of its own, at least to the degree that it is able. It gives the appearance of caring for her welfare and will not tolerate having her taken away."

I stared at him. "So what do you want me to do?"

A siren chirped in the distance as another firetruck pulled onto the lot. The humans were persistent, I'd give them that. At this point, I would've just let the building burn.

Judge Engle glanced toward it and then continued, "The procedure on Miss Moreau is not complete. We believe we were partially successful, but we were interrupted before we could finish—something which undoubtedly has left her in an unstable and vulnerable state. However, not all of our stores of the Beast's magic were destroyed in its attempt to flee us today, nor was all of our equipment, and thus the process can continue. You must get the enforcers close to her. They will take care of the rest."

So I was a babysitter. A representative for the Judiciary to keep those zombie-like snakes in suits under control till they could find poor little Ariabella.

Anger began to boil inside me. I was worth more than this. I was the son of Irene Marseilles, for pity's sake, and the best damn novitiate that they had by far. If this was so important, why weren't they sending a judge?

The answer presented itself almost immediately. They didn't think I was *actually* one of them. They hadn't committed too many resources to me.

They thought I was expendable.

"This is a vital position, Mister Marseilles."

I tensed, realizing the bastard must have seen something of my thoughts in my expression. Swiftly, I obliterated any trace of dissent from my face.

Beside us, the ambulance shuddered slightly when the driver shifted into gear, and the engine rumble changed to a low growl as the vehicle pulled away.

"There is more at stake than you realize," Judge Engle continued. "Others are after the girl—others who may try to co-opt what we've undertaken with her and use it for themselves." His attention slid to the ambulance driving toward the exit. "There are traitors in our midst. Agents of subversive forces who have been allying against us for nearly a century and who seek nothing but our destruction. The very Judiciary could be in danger."

My temper cooled fast, turning to buried alarm. My mother had never hinted at anything like *this*.

"You will be well rewarded for assisting us now."

I dipped my head in an obedient nod.

He twitched his head in acceptance. "We wish you to start

by searching for hiding places where someone in Miss Moreau's potential condition would feel the least threatened. Roadside motels, for example, rather than truck stops or highway rest areas. We would like you to focus your efforts on areas to the north, preferably at several hours' distance from here."

My confused curiosity didn't touch my face this time. He sounded like they already knew where she was heading.

"The enforcers will explain more on the way. They are waiting at the far side of the warehouse lot."

I knew a dismissal when I heard it and I was smart enough not to push for more information. He wouldn't tell me anything anyway. "Yes, sir. Thank you, sir."

Without another word, I strode away from the destruction of the warehouse, my thoughts turning fully to myself and dismissing the judge as effectively as he had dismissed me.

My fists clenched till I could feel my knuckles straining. The Beast had killed my *mother*. With one act, it had transformed me from the *son* of Irene Marseilles to the *orphan* of Irene Marseilles. And sure, I could manipulate that. Pity was a wonderful leverage point with most people. But it meant any benefit I would have gotten out of my mother's activities and her escalation through the Judiciary's ranks had been cut short the moment it killed her.

It was practically *sabotage*.

I stalked toward the enforcers standing around a black sedan at the opposite end of the parking lot. It was sabotage. It really was. But then, everything wasn't lost. The Judiciary hadn't dumped me by the roadside. They still thought they could use me, so that meant I could use them. And the question remained of how human the Beast really was. The creature actually believed it cared for Ari, and distance from her caused it pain. I could use that too.

Oh, I could use the *hell* out of that.

My lip twitched in an icy smile. I'd find them. I'd track them down and let the enforcers do whatever they were going to do to Ari.

Eventually.

But in the meantime, that creature had a weakness, and that weakness was my little hobby. The judges were right: I'd studied Ari. I knew what she cared about. I knew what—and who—mattered to her. Getting inside someone's head didn't work nearly as well if you didn't pay attention.

I'd find her. I'd make her suffer and watch that creature suffer too. I'd make them both *beg* for a way to pay me back for how they'd taken my mother—and thus every advantage for which I'd planned to use her—away from me.

And then I'd see if there wasn't some way to make that ancient monster die.

My smile grew. This was going to be fun.

2

ARI

The motel room was crowded with four other people and a thunderstorm, and barring the storm, I didn't know a single one of them.

"Okay, we're here," a guy with golden brown hair snapped, shutting the front door. "Now, what the hell is going on?"

Noah glanced to me. A supernatural thunderstorm in the form of a human, he didn't need to breathe, and probably wouldn't have been breathing anyway, even if oxygen were necessary to him. Even after I sat down on the musty bed, he remained standing by my side like a bodyguard, every bit as tense as me.

I could tell. The empathic connection between us was practically vibrating.

A pale-skinned brunette girl took a seat on the second bed, waiting for our answer. A girl with olive skin and large brown eyes sat next to her. A third girl, suntanned and blond, leaned against the television stand, studying us all with a wary expression.

"You didn't say a word in the car," the brunette pressed. "Neither of you." Her gaze flicked over the t-shirt and jean shorts she'd given me. They covered the green-scaled one-piece I hoped she still thought was a swimsuit, instead of the magically altered skin that it actually was. "I understand if you don't want to talk about what happened, but please just tell us if you're okay?"

I looked up at Noah. I didn't want to answer her. Even if I couldn't remember her name or find a single memory of how she fit into my life, Noah had told me she was my cousin. Something inside me was desperate to avoid seeing hurt or fear in her eyes.

"No," Noah replied quietly. "Ari's not."

The empathic connection between us darkened with anger and pain. He hated telling my family about the hell the judges had put me through. What they'd taken. What they'd changed. He wanted to make the judges pay, to fix this once and for all, not explain to the others what the leaders of the ruanir had done. I was part dehaian now—or strakirin or whatever. My body would transform if I let it, or if I lost control of it, turning me into a scaled creature with an eel tail and brutally sharp spikes on my arms.

That wasn't all. The judges hadn't only changed my body. They'd come within seconds of destroying me completely. I'd been exposed to their "enhancements," magical procedures designed to obliterate my mind and alter everything I was. Had they succeeded, I would have been made into a new form of enforcer—a creature with no memory of her former life, whose sole purpose was to serve the judges and whose slightest touch could kill.

I was a monster. I had no idea how to tell anyone that. Neither did he.

"What did they do?" The olive-skinned girl's tone was direct, almost clinical, like she needed to cut to the heart of this without delay. It might have seemed uncaring, except for the worry I could see in her eyes.

Noah shook his head. "They, um… they…"

"They tried to make me like the enforcers," I supplied, forcing out the words.

Silence greeted the statement.

"What?" the guy demanded.

"The enforcers," I repeated, suddenly wary. "You know—"

"I know what they *are*," the guy snapped. "I want to know what they—"

His face went dead with shock. A panicked noise left the brunette girl.

"Oh God," whispered the olive-skinned girl next to her. She let out a sharp breath, like she was attempting to regain her equilibrium. "Ari, when you say they *tried*, do you mean they—"

"It's all gone," Noah confirmed quietly. "She remembers me, what they did, maybe anyone or anything that was around her when it happened, but…"

The brunette pressed her hand to the brown bedspread, steadying herself. She looked like someone had punched her in the stomach and what color had been in her pale skin drained entirely. Her other hand fumbled into the olive-skinned girl's as if seeking support.

I turned my face from the sight. It hurt all the more because I couldn't even remember why.

"I'm sorry," I said softly.

A choked gasp left the guy. He looked like he was going to be sick.

I scrambled for something to help. "Maybe if you told me your names, it'd—"

The guy's fist slammed back into the door hard enough to dent the cheap metal. I jumped and my forearms stung as spikes tried to rush from them. Frantic, I clutched my arms to my middle, begging the horrible defenses not to emerge.

The tingling faded. I remembered how to breathe.

"You should have let us come with you," the guy hissed to Noah. "You shouldn't have just—"

"Jace," the olive-skinned girl cut in.

"How could you let them do this to her! *How?*" He strode toward Noah. "You son of a bitch. Everything you are and you couldn't stop *this?*"

I scrambled up between them. "He tried, okay? Noah saved me. He did. It almost killed him to do it, but he did."

The guy stared at me.

"Jace, right? Jace, I'm trying. I swear to *God* that I am trying. It's just taking a while, is all."

His expression crumpled into anguish. "Ari…"

The word hurt. A sob crushed my chest at its sound. "We're going to fix this," I promised him. "Okay? We are. We just—"

He turned away, raking his hands through his light brown hair like he wanted to rip it out. I stared after him, a pained feeling stabbing through me, and then my focus turned to the others. No one else was looking at me either, and it felt intentional, like all of them were avoiding my eyes. I floundered, aching and lost in this room full of people who were supposedly my family, and whom I didn't even know.

Noah's hand found mine and a thread of comfort ran through our connection. It steadied me. I pressed a hand to my face, smudging away the tears that had welled up.

"There is one other thing," Noah said.

Jace looked like he wanted to kill him. "What?"

Noah didn't react to the expression. "Your mother."

"What about her?"

"The judges said she volunteered Ari. Offered her to them for this in exchange for their favor."

Jace stared at him, expressions racing across his face that I couldn't read. Twitching slightly, his lip appeared on the edge of an incredulous scoff, but his gray eyes were like ice. "She did *what?*"

"They said your mother brought Ari to that party specifically to give Ari to them. The whole event was a setup. Some kind of plan to get me and Ari near each other. They said something about your mother spending the year giving Ari drugs, priming her to absorb magic from me. That she couldn't have avoided it."

Jace turned away again. On the opposite bed, the brunette looked nauseated. The olive-skinned girl stared at the floor as if struggling to wrap her head around what she'd heard.

"That judge," the blond girl said into the silence. "Maia's father."

"Yeah," Noah answered. "That's where we're headed next."

Jace made an angry noise. "Then what the hell are we *here* for? Let's go."

"Not yet," Noah said.

Jace's fists clenched like he wanted to come at him again.

"I think the judges tracked the SUV," Noah continued. "They watched Santa Lucina because they know Chloe likes to visit it and they thought I might meet her there. But they found us even when we were at Baylie's place. They must have seen the SUV."

"They know about Chloe?" the blond girl asked.

"Yeah, but I don't think they know about you. Jace, they only mentioned that I was connected to the Yvarian king's girlfriend, right? Not Baylie?"

Jace scowled. "Yeah."

Noah nodded. "It had to be the SUV, then."

I glanced between him and the blond girl, surprised. He had an empathic connection to her too?

"So what's the plan?" the brunette girl asked.

"Travel at night," Noah replied. "Stay off the main highway. And until then…" He shrugged. "What Ari said. Names. Places. Anything you can do to try to help her remember."

The brunette nodded. She motioned quickly for me to come sit on the bed with her, as if every second we wasted might mean a smaller chance my memory could be saved.

I worried she might be right.

Still watching Noah, I circled to the other bed. Jace stood by the window, his back to the room like he had retreated into his own world. The blond girl, Baylie, skirted by us and headed for Noah, that wary expression still on her face.

I sank onto the thin, quilted bedspread. The brunette tried for a smile, mostly failing.

"So, um…" She seemed like she was fighting tears. "I-I'm Maia. Um, Maia Davenport. Your cousin. This is Dhanya, uh, Singh, my fiancée. We got engaged last week. You're going to be my maid of honor."

A breath pressed from my chest at the hope in her eyes, at the fear in her voice. I knew that I'd been there. That I'd known this. I could see it on her face, the reality that'd existed only days before.

Now there was nothing.

"I'm sorry," I said. "I can't—"

"It's okay," Dhanya cut in, her tone calm and certain. She took Maia's hand, squeezing it. "We'll just keep talking. It'll come back."

I nodded, desperate to believe her. Drawing a steadying breath, I set myself to memorizing details of the life I'd forgotten.

3

NOAH

From the corner of my eye, I watched Ari. Sitting on the bed, she focused on Maia and Dhanya with a quivering sort of intensity, like she was trying to burn the details of everything they said into her brain by sheer force of will. For their part, they were holding it together, though Maia still looked like she wanted to cry. Jace hadn't turned around. He stood, staring stone-like out the window.

Meanwhile, I wanted to find those judge bastards and make them remember in vivid detail *exactly* why they'd spent centuries hiding from the Beast.

I closed my eyes, fighting down the rage. It wouldn't help Ari. She needed to concentrate right now.

"Noah?" Baylie asked quietly. "Can I talk to you?"

It was hard to keep from grimacing. I'd known this was coming, and honestly, I needed to speak to her too.

But that didn't make it any less awkward.

"Yeah."

I glanced at Jace. He still hadn't moved.

"Outside?" I suggested, keeping my voice low.

She nodded. Her gaze darted to Ari and the others, and then she headed out of the room. I followed, tugging the now-dented door closed behind us.

Baylie walked down the sidewalk toward the SUV and then rounded on me as soon as she reached it. "Are you okay?"

I hesitated. Of all the questions I thought she wanted to ask, that hadn't been the one I'd expected, although in reality, I probably should have.

"Yeah."

"Really? Because I—"

"I'm fine," I cut in, not wanting to talk about it.

She paused. "Then is that what I think it is? On Ari. That 'swimsuit' thing?"

I checked around to make sure none of the others had come outside where they might hear us. "Yeah."

"She's *dehaian?*" Baylie whispered. "They took her memory and made her—"

"No."

Baylie waited.

"She's something else," I explained uncomfortably. "They called it strakirin. Some experiment the judges are running. I've never seen anything like it. But I don't think she's ready for her family to know that."

Baylie looked down the length of the motel as if she could see the others in the room.

"Just keep it quiet for now, okay?" I asked her.

She hesitated before nodding.

I forced myself to continue. "There's something I need to talk to you about too."

She glanced back to me.

"I need to warn Zeke," I told her. "There was a dehaian at that lab, one who worked with the judges to set Yvaria up. And he's not the only one. Some dehaians also made it look like Zeke's soldiers attacked a party last week and killed several ruanir. The judges said something about rallying their people against Yvaria. I think they're trying to start a war."

I paused. This was going to be the hard part. "Which is where I need your help. I can't leave Ari. This connection… too much distance between us still hurts. So I need you to go back and get in touch with Chloe and have her talk to Zeke. Warn him since I can't. Please."

She stared at me. "You want me to… Noah, I'm not going to *leave*."

"We can't keep them in the dark about this, Baylie. I don't know what the judges' plan is, but Chloe and Zeke are in danger. They have to be. These guys want a war, and with what they did to Ari…" I shook my head. "They drained something from me, something they were going to keep giving to her. And since it was whatever the hell she took from me that *started* this whole mess, I can't guarantee the judges won't begin again and try this on someone else. Zeke has to know what's going on."

Baylie turned away.

"Please," I pressed.

She exhaled, her teeth grinding. "No."

"Baylie—"

"No, I'm not leaving you! Listen, you need me. If it wasn't for me, you'd still be on that beach, probably with those enforcer things closing in."

I fought to keep from scowling at her. I would've figured something out, found someplace Ari could hide until we could contact Maia or Dhanya, since both of them probably still had their cell phones. Or I would've convinced Ari to go back into the ocean. It would've been fine.

"Noah, I can help," Baylie insisted. "I'll call Diane. Ask her to look for the dehaians. Chloe and Zeke always leave a few people stationed on the beach these days, in case we need to get in touch with them while they're underwater. If they see your stepmom looking around, they'll come talk to her. She can tell them your message, okay?"

"It'll go faster if you're there."

"How?"

"One less person to pass the information through. If you have to talk to Diane first—"

Baylie scoffed. "That's ridiculous. It'll take ten seconds to tell Diane what to say."

"Maybe, but—"

"Maybe nothing. You're being silly."

"No, I just—"

"What, you think I can't—"

"Dammit, I don't want you to come!"

She stopped. I looked away.

"These bastards are dangerous, okay?" I worked to make my voice calmer. "I don't want you or anyone else involved. I appreciate how you helped—and you *did*—but please, let me keep you out of this."

She was silent for a moment. "What happened?" she asked, her voice carefully controlled. "Back wherever they had Ari, before you took off for the ocean?"

I didn't respond.

"Because Noah, it felt…" A breath left her. "It felt like you were *dying*. Like I could *feel* you dying in my mind. And Ari said—" Baylie closed her eyes for a second. "You claim you're okay, but I haven't picked up on pain from you like that since… *ever*. Not even when they linked you two together. Because that wasn't her this time, right? That was you."

I struggled for a response. I couldn't get into that. The judges had built a trap specifically designed to drain whatever magic Ari needed from me, and then to kill me when they were through. It would've worked, if not for Ari destroying the machines with her own powers.

I didn't remember much of the rest. The part of me that was the Beast had taken over long before the cage walls came down. I remembered people screaming, remembered lifting Ari out of that place while the ceiling crashed to the ground. Everything else was a blur of rage and pain from what the judges had been doing to us.

I should've known Baylie would feel it all.

"I don't want you involved," I repeated.

She exhaled roughly, like she was holding back tears. "So I'm right."

"We can call Diane and Dad, have them come pick you up.

We're going to be here for a few hours so that should give them a chance to—"

She turned and started back toward the motel room.

"Baylie!" I grabbed her arm. She yanked it away. "Baylie, you can't—"

"You don't tell me what I can't do!" She glared at me. "I'm not leaving. You're my family. I'm not going to simply sit at home and hope everything turns out alright." She trembled, furious. "I had to do that last year."

I stared at her, frozen for a moment, but I couldn't meet her eyes for long.

"I am going with you," she insisted.

"You—"

"It's done!" Her voice broke. "Okay, Noah? End of discussion."

I wanted to keep arguing. Of anyone here, she could get the most hurt. She wasn't like me. She didn't have magic like Ari or Jace or the others. She was human and vulnerable and I wanted to protect her.

Especially since she was my family.

"Come on." Baylie motioned toward the motel room. "We can't just stay out here."

"I hate this," I told her.

"Makes two of us, then." She started toward the door, pulling out her cell to call Diane as she went.

Biting back the urge to swear vehemently at her, at myself, at the entire situation, I followed.

～ 4 ～

ARI

My life felt like a puzzle and I was missing half the pieces.

I shifted position on the bed, listening to Maia recount a story from my childhood. It'd become clear early on that parts of my memory were intact, though in strange fashions. I remembered traveling cross country with Noah, remembered being at Judge Engle's party when the dehaians attacked. I even remembered growing up in Arizona and moving to stay in Chicago, though I didn't know with whom I'd lived before that or why I'd had to go. Maia and Dhanya were likewise missing, and Jace wasn't in my memories at all. It was as if someone had scrubbed out their images with an eraser and reset all the scenes of my life, leaving empty spaces where nearly everyone had been standing.

It was terrifying.

"—so then Jace gave you the toy *he'd* won at the fair," Maia said, "and you stopped crying."

I winced. "Well, that's embarrassing."

"Oh come on, you were three."

I shrugged, glancing to the others. Noah sat by the window in a rickety metal chair, watching the parking lot through a slender gap in the thick curtains. Even if he didn't move a muscle, I could still feel his amusement. On the edge of the other bed, Baylie looked away from the television, eyeing him like she'd picked up on it too.

"You know," she commented to me, "I heard that Noah did something similar when his mom and dad took him to an amusement park as a kid. Only I'm *pretty* sure he didn't stop crying."

"Hey, what?" Noah protested, turning. "Who told you that?"

Baylie grinned. "Maddox." She glanced to us. "His older brother."

"Yeah, well." Noah shifted his shoulders uncomfortably. "Let's just keep the focus on Ari here, alright?"

He went back to the window. Baylie looked to me, still grinning.

I couldn't help but smile. I liked Noah's stepsister. It'd been strange at first to think that someone else in the room had a connection to him similar to mine. I'd wondered if she could tell anything about me through it, though I mostly doubted it. I had no idea about her. She seemed nice, though. She'd been quiet for most of the morning, and the aggravation in Noah after he'd come back from that short time outside made it feel like they'd had an argument. But as the day went on, they both seemed to let it go. Over the past few hours, she'd interrupted us numerous times with jokes, doing her best to keep things from getting too depressing.

I had no words for how much I appreciated it.

The television screen changed as the local news started up. The camera panned over images of a destroyed warehouse, its walls caved in and its roof scattered in chunks of debris across the parking lot. Quickly, Baylie thumbed off the remote, blanking the screen.

I dropped my gaze to the brown, quilted bedspread. I didn't remember much of what happened when Noah and I had escaped the judges, only crashing sounds amid the darkness of his other form. But we'd already seen the images on the news during lunch today. From what reporters said, the authorities suspected the damage was the result of a gas explosion or some kind of chemical being stored there. Nearby workers claimed to have seen a cloud of smoke billowing up, though it had disappeared with incredible speed. Several bodies had been found in the wreckage, but the police were withholding names.

I shivered. The more distance we could get between ourselves and that place, the better.

The front door opened. Jace came in. "SUV's packed," he said flatly. "It'll be full dark in another few minutes so we should probably get going."

Dhanya nodded. She and Maia climbed off the bed. I followed, my gaze darting to Jace as I passed. He'd scarcely said a word to anyone all day. He'd barely even looked at anyone, me included.

Maybe me especially.

Discomfort made my stomach churn. Maia and Dhanya said he was my brother. From the sound of their stories, we were close. But maybe close didn't mean we talked much.

Or even looked at each other much.

I pushed the thought away. I had no memories to go on. I was probably making a big deal out of nothing.

The others were silent while we got into the SUV. Noah took one of the fold-down seats in the far back, his legs propped on either side of the bags on the floor. I joined him while the others found places in the middle and front of the vehicle. Jace climbed behind the wheel. He'd taken a nap earlier in the day, in preparation for driving through most of the night. The sky was black by the time we reached the highway, and as the hours crept on, the others gradually drifted off to sleep.

I felt like Jace's eyes were on me in the rearview mirror, though every time I looked up, he was only watching the highway.

The miles blurred one into the other. Splashes of white city lights glared in my eyes only to vanish back into black oblivion between towns. The faint rumble of the tires swallowed the quiet sounds the others made in their sleep, leaving only a low, white-noise hum that did nothing to lull me into unconsciousness.

Maybe that was a good thing.

My attention drifted over a small town as we passed. Closed shops, their outside lights still glowing in the night. A truck stop with a few lonely cars in its parking lot, even at this hour. Houses with darkened windows and empty yards, each one carrying a dreamlike quality, as if the homes were resting along with their occupants.

I looked away. I didn't want to sleep. I didn't want nightmares in which the few memories I still possessed could rear their horrible heads. The judges. The tank they'd trapped me in. The things they did to my body. I knew I'd have to rest eventually, but for the moment—

A weird feeling thrummed through me, like a compass needle suddenly vibrating in my head. I snapped back to alertness, my discomfort faltering into alarm. Something was pulling at me out there. Tugging at me like invisible threads attached to my skin, my mind, my entire body. And somehow, I knew exactly what the sensation was pointing toward.

The ocean.

Shivers crept over my skin. I could *feel* the *ocean*. Its presence. There, over the horizon between those two hills was the closest place to—and now it had shifted. It was closer there now. Beyond the gas station we'd just passed and now—

I wanted to throw up.

"Ari?" Noah whispered. "You okay?"

Not even close.

"What is it?" he asked, reading into my silence.

I glanced to Jace quickly. He wasn't looking at us. I couldn't tell if he'd heard Noah. "The ocean," I whispered back. "I can… I can tell where the ocean, um… where it's—" At the expression on Noah's face, I stopped. "What is this?"

"Dehaian trait," he admitted. "No matter where they are on land, they still know where to find the closest access to the ocean."

I trembled.

"It's okay," Noah said. "There's bound to be a few things they…"

He trailed off, picking up on how the words were affecting me.

I fought the urge to look back toward the ocean I knew was there—right there, beyond that stand of trees was the nearest point now—even if we were miles from the water.

"What else?" I asked tightly.

"Ari, I don't—"

"What? I know they have spikes. I know they have magic that can make you fall in love with them. I know…" The sick feeling grew. I really wasn't tired. Hungry, either.

And dehaians barely needed to eat or sleep. They could go for days without both, if necessary. Instead, they could live off of magic. Ocean magic. It sustained them.

Oh God, I was probably—

"Ari." Noah moved to take my hand. I flinched back. He froze, alarmed.

I stared at him, my mouth moving for a moment before it managed to make a sound. "I'm not tired. I haven't been hungry all day."

Understanding filtered through the connection between us. "Maybe it's just nerves."

I nodded, clinging to the words even though I could tell he didn't believe them.

Noah knew what this was, same as I did.

"What about those stories?" he asked, clearly trying to change the subject. "Did they help at all?"

My stomach twisted tighter.

He grimaced, feeling my tension. "Give it time. I'm sure it'll… you know."

I looked away. I would've given anything for him to be able to lie to me right now.

The SUV rolled through the darkness. The closest point of the ocean kept shifting in my head, skipping along first here, then here, then over there…

And some part of me wanted to go toward it.

My hand found Noah's of its own accord. He tensed, wary questioning coming through to me.

I didn't move. He wasn't like what I felt on the other side of the horizon. He… he seemed different. He had ocean magic, *was* ocean magic, yet somehow it wasn't the same.

But what he was had changed me. Made me like this. Baylie's friend, Ellie, had said that what the judges had done to me fed upon the connection between us.

I shivered. Maybe that was true, but his connection to me had also saved my life. Broken through what the judges had been doing to my mind, back in that lab. I was fairly certain traces of his magic had been slipping through to me when I'd been in the water yesterday, and maybe that had been part of what helped me return to looking like a human.

Whatever the judges had wanted his magic to do to me, I knew on some gut-deep level that things weren't going the way they planned.

Noah was somehow responsible for that.

His fingers tightened on mine. I closed my eyes. I'd be okay.

I would. We'd make Maia's father fix this, all of this, no matter *what* it took to convince him to do so.

I only had to hang on until then.

The sky was still dark when we pulled into the parking lot of another motel, though the clouds were beginning to become visible and the world seemed to promise sunrise within the next hour or so. Without a word, Baylie climbed out and then waited for Noah to join her before she headed for the front desk. The supply of cash Jace, Maia, and Dhanya had brought with them was running perilously low, and for the past few hundred miles, we'd been using Baylie's debit card to get by.

I knew Noah hated it, but there wasn't any choice. The judges had never seen Baylie and most likely had never known in which apartment we'd been hiding when they kidnapped me off the street. They didn't know Noah's name, either—they thought his human form was some shape chosen for the Beast by Chloe—which meant they couldn't look up his family or friends. Thus, they were almost certainly still unaware of his stepsister, leaving her as the only one of us who probably wasn't being tracked.

Hopefully, anyway.

Baylie and Noah returned a minute later, a room key in hand. We drove down to the furthest door from the road.

The room was stark, without a single scrap of cheap art on the white, pebbled surface of the walls. The bedspreads bore faded and nondescript patterns that my eyes wanted to slide over, and the mirror on the wall beside the bathroom was nothing more than a small square of glass in plastic clips.

But it seemed clean, for all that it looked like a prison cell.

Maia set her bag on the nearest bed. "You going to get some sleep, Jace?"

He shrugged. "Yeah, maybe." He headed for the bathroom.

Maia watched him go, and then caught me studying them both. She tried to smile. "Want to talk some more?"

"Sure," I agreed, though I really didn't feel like it. I hadn't been able to close my eyes all night, and even now, I wasn't remotely tired.

It was unnerving.

I nudged the bag aside and sat down next to her.

"So Dhanya's told me some of what they do to enforcers," Maia started, "and I'm thinking maybe that could help."

I hesitated, eyeing Maia and Dhanya warily. "How does she know about enforcers?"

"Her uncles and a number of her cousins all became that, after her grandmother died from exposure to ocean magic."

I looked to Dhanya in surprise.

"Happened through a friend she'd had since childhood," Dhanya supplied, a touch uncomfortably. "Nothing anyone could do, not by then. But my family figured that if someone could've been there, caught that friend before they poisoned others, then maybe my grandmother would've still been with us. My uncles, cousins, all of them signed up for the conversion process after her death." She paused. "I did too."

I blinked, alarmed. "But—"

"I changed my mind."

I hesitated, not sure I should press. Yet even with my memory gone, I had a vague sense that people didn't back out of becoming an enforcer.

That almost no one did.

"Why?" I asked.

She shrugged. "I met Maia."

I waited.

Dhanya drew a breath, shifting around a bit. "I'd planned on joining. I'd taken several of the classes at the training center, been put through a dozen tests for compatibility with the process. My cousins were a few months ahead of me in the program, so I'd seen what they were studying, what changes they went through. And, yeah…" She picked at a piece of loose stitching on the bedspread. "It bothered me, I guess. The way we'd lose our identity. Our memories." Her gaze flicked my direction. Discomfort burned through me. "But I thought it was the responsible thing to do, if it meant more families wouldn't have to suffer because of someone else's mistake."

It took me a moment to find my voice. "And now?" I asked tightly. She was here, so obviously—well, *hopefully*—she didn't agree with what the judges had done to me or think I should have submitted to what they wanted me to become.

But maybe she did.

Dhanya looked up at me. "Now I think it's bullshit. You didn't ask for this. Even the *Beast* didn't ask for this. Now I'm reeling from relief that I *didn't* give up my identity, my will, everything, to serve those bastards when this isn't *anything* like the Judiciary I thought I knew my whole life."

I relaxed. I could understand that. Even if I couldn't remember her before now… I could understand how she felt. I'd feel the same way, if it was someone else in my position.

Dhanya reached over, lacing her fingers through Maia's. "I chose not to become an enforcer because I met the love of my life. Because from the moment I laid eyes on Maia, I felt things I'd never felt with anyone else. I felt *home*. And suddenly, joining the enforcers wasn't just about avenging my grandmother or defending my family… It meant giving up someone I loved like I'd never loved anyone before. I knew I wouldn't remember her if I went through the conversion process, but… it's not always perfect, that process, so what if some part of me did? What if some part of me knew what I'd lost… forever? And even if it *did* work and I didn't remember… I wasn't ready to let who I was die anymore."

She sighed. "My family wasn't happy about my decision. Some of them, anyway. My relatives have always had powerful positions in the ruanir community, but for so many of us to join raised my family's position even higher. A few understood my choice, though."

I hesitated. I was glad for her. I was. But I was also seeing parallels to myself in what she'd said a moment before, and the possibility made my stomach quiver with tremulous hope. "What about the enforcers the process doesn't work on? The ones who still have some memories?"

Dhanya didn't respond.

"Is there, like, a cure or…?"

She wetted her lips. "They're killed. Or kept." She wouldn't meet my eyes. "Some because they're still useful. Most for experimentation into what went wrong. It depends."

My stomach turned to lead. *Nauseated* lead.

"But just because the judges do that, doesn't mean it's the only option," Dhanya continued. "If the memories are buried rather than destroyed, then there's a chance we could trigger them somehow."

I'd thought that's what we'd already been doing.

"We may have been going too broad," Dhanya said like she read my expression. "If we narrow our focus, search *specifically* for small details that could serve as triggers, maybe we could uncover more of your memories. For example, you could visualize what Maia describes, little things. Toys or dishes or decorations or whatever comes to mind. Perhaps those will kickstart a connection to other memories."

I hesitated. Maia looked so hopeful at her fiancée's words. Desperate and hopeful.

And I'd definitely already been doing that.

"What if Ari tried saying more of what she remembers?" Noah offered.

I glanced over. His expression was so carefully blank, it was obvious to me that he'd picked up on my reaction.

"In addition, I mean," he continued. "Trade back and forth, her telling you stories and then you filling in the details?"

Maia nodded. "Yeah. Yeah, sure."

She turned to me. I searched for any memory.

It was difficult. They were all bits and pieces. Nothing fit together in any way that made sense. "I remember, um, being in a desert. Maybe near some mountains? I think there might've been a tent, but I'm not—"

Jace came back out of the bathroom. I stopped.

"One of the camping trips," Maia supplied eagerly. "Your dad used to take you both on those."

Without a word, Jace strode past us, heading out of the room.

"Hey, Jace?" Maia tried. "Maybe you could help—"

Jace yanked the door open.

A balding man with a fringe of brown hair stood there, his hand raised to knock. "Oh. Hi."

"What the—" Jace slammed the door.

A knock came. "Excuse me?" the man called.

Alarmed, Jace turned to us. "Who the hell—"

"I take it you don't know him?" Baylie seemed torn between anxiety and something approaching relief.

Which made sense. Everyone they knew seemed connected to the judges.

I shivered, fighting to keep spikes from emerging on my arms.

"He doesn't *look* like an enforcer," Dhanya allowed, though from her tone, she didn't sound certain that mattered.

"Maybe he's with the motel?" Maia suggested.

Noah crossed to the door. Eyeing him, Jace retreated. Noah took the handle and then pulled the door open.

"Yeah?" he asked.

"Um, hi." The man smoothed his tweed jacket nervously. "I'm, uh, I'm a salesman for Bixby Tires and I saw that your SUV needed—"

"We're not interested." Noah moved to shut the door.

"Oh no, please!" The man shoved a pamphlet at him, which became pinned in the closed door. Scowling, Noah tugged it out.

A white business card fell from inside, something scribbled on its back. Noah bent and picked it up.

He froze, alarm racing through him.

My breath caught. "What?"

Radiating caution, Noah opened the door a second time. The man stood where he'd been, anxiously rocking his weight from one foot to the other.

"Talk," Noah ordered.

I shivered at the threat in his voice.

"What's going on?" Jace demanded.

Noah extended the card without looking away from the man. Jace took it. Rage surged across his face.

He dropped the card and shoved past Noah to reach the guy.

"No," the man protested, "You don't need to—"

Jace grabbed him and yanked him into the motel room. Noah stepped back quickly, keeping an eye to the outside, and then shut the door while Jace slammed the man against the wall beside it.

"Who are you?" Jace snapped.

"Guys?" Maia asked. "What did it say?"

Baylie shoved up from the other bed and retrieved the card from the floor. Watching Jace and Noah, she retreated to our side, showing us the card.

Pencil scratches formed hastily scrawled words.

They know where you're going.

My blood went cold. A stinging sensation spread through my forearms. The judges. This had to mean the judges.

Spikes pushed through the skin of my forearms, the blades sharp and translucent and utterly driven by adrenaline. I couldn't stop them. I couldn't even breathe. The others would see them at any moment.

Baylie dropped the note and strode past me. She snagged a pillow from the bed and then shoved it into my lap. I tucked my arms beneath it, looking up at her in surprise. She knew about me. And clearly, she also knew I didn't want the others to find out.

I could have hugged her if my arms wouldn't have given everything away.

Maia and Dhanya stared at us both, appearing shocked and confused but not like they'd seen me turning into a monster. "What—" Dhanya started.

"Nothing." Baylie spun back toward the little man. "Answer his question. Who are you?"

Red-faced with alarm, the man sputtered. "P-please, I—"

Jace thrust the little man against the wall harder. "Now!"

"Harvey Stolberg. I-I'm Harvey Stolberg. I—"

"What the hell is that note?" Jace snapped.

The man winced at the sight of the card on the floor. "I,

um… Oh dear. I can explain. I only—"

Another knock came on the door.

Harvey turned his head toward it. "You—"

Jace's hand clamped over the man's mouth. Noah glanced to him and then inched the door open.

"Morning," came a young woman's voice.

A grunt followed, like she'd shoved at the door. Noah didn't budge a millimeter. A thud came next, like a boot hitting the cheap wood.

"Open up!" Another thud followed, harder than the first. "You want someone calling the cops? You can't just haul someone into your room and not expect—"

Noah stepped back. A young woman with a ponytail of fiery red hair stumbled into the entryway, unbalanced like she'd been midway through kicking the door again. Straightening fast, she swept her gaze over Jace, Noah and the rest of us, a predatory look in her pale blue eyes.

"Let him go," she ordered Jace, keeping her distance from him and Noah.

"Like hell," Jace snapped.

Ignoring them, Noah checked outside and then shut the door.

The girl's face turned a furious shade of crimson. "I *said,* let him—"

"Do it," Noah interrupted.

Jace eyed him briefly and then released Harvey with a shove.

The girl glanced from Noah to Jace. "You okay, Harvey?"

Adjusting his tweed jacket, Harvey cleared his throat. "Fine,

fine. Just a misunderstanding."

Her attention flicked over us next, pausing at the pillow on my lap and then the business card. At the sight of the card, a scowl crossed her face as if something clicked and she didn't like it. "A *note*? Dammit, Harvey…"

"I couldn't know who else might be in the room!" the man sputtered. "I wasn't trying—"

"Who the hell are you people?" Jace interrupted.

The girl turned a glare on him. Tall and appearing to be about Jace's age, she looked like a model for chic army surplus in her fitted, gray t-shirt, black combat boots and cargo pants. The fact that she was gorgeous didn't hurt the impression either. But the threat in her baby blue eyes dispelled the image, making her seem more like a tiger debating whether to strike.

"Willa Blackwood," she allowed. "We've been looking for you."

Jace appeared like he couldn't care less. "That doesn't answer—"

"And we're friends of Adam Moreau."

Jace tensed and Maia did too. I glanced between them, alarmed. Moreau was my last name. And Adam… Adam was…

The memory slipped from my grasp like smoke.

"He's dead," Jace said, not taking his eyes from Willa.

"Yeah. We know."

Silence stretched.

"Who's this we're talking about?" Noah asked cautiously.

"Their dad," Maia supplied when Jace didn't answer.

A quiver ran through me. Wait, that was my *father's* name?

I'd forgotten my own father's—

Noah's eyes twitched to me. I swallowed hard, struggling to smother my horror so we both could concentrate.

"What do you have to do with him?" Jace demanded.

Willa glanced across us all again. "Everyone here good?" she asked him.

"All ruanir, yeah."

Jace's cold tone was level. I kept my eyes on the girl, not daring to let them go to Baylie or, worse, Noah.

Willa studied us a moment more as if weighing whether to trust the response. "Adam Moreau worked for us," she said finally. "*With* us. You all are a part of something bigger than just the few of you. A *lot* bigger." She paused. "Your father ever mention the Breakmire Initiative?"

Jace shook his head.

Willa glanced to Harvey.

"If they're helping Ariabella and her brother," the man offered, "there's an eighty-four percent probability that they're safe."

"They shoved you against a wall."

"Eighty-three, then."

She regarded him flatly before turning back to Jace. "Your father was set to be a judge. His father had been one and his brother became one. He was supposed to do the same. But instead, he became an artist, and took his children around the country in pursuit of his passion. That was the story and, I'm guessing, what you all believed. The truth was far different. Adam Moreau was a leader in a secret movement within the ruanir people—one the judges want to see destroyed at any cost. He was a high-ranking member of the resistance."

I stared at her. Jace did the same. I couldn't remember my father and my childhood was like a confetti of shredded photographs with most of the parts missing, but from Jace's expression I could tell he hadn't known this either.

A resistance against the judges. It seemed impossible. *Suicidal.*

"Bullshit," Jace said. "There's no such thing."

"And we're happy for everyone to keep believing that. It lets us continue working toward our goal of destroying the hold the judges have on our people without any Judiciary loyalist do-gooders trying to turn us in."

"What are you talking about?" I asked.

Willa's blue eyes flicked to me briefly. "There's a war going on," she said, "though many ruanir don't realize it. In certain parts of our society, the Judiciary is seen as a necessary entity, a protective force. They guard us from ocean magic, serve as a policing body against any who would tell the world of our existence, and they help those who don't have the money to hide from human notice. But the reality is far different. The wealthy ruanir live in a bubble, convinced the judges protect them. Convinced that, no matter how terrifying the enforcers or the judges can be, this is the best system for all of us. Meanwhile, those ruanir who *aren't* rich, who haven't been able to keep their money for one reason or another, are *owned* by the Judiciary. They move when the judges say move, work where the judges say work. They do *whatever* the Judiciary orders, and the rich ruanir think it's all for their own protection. But the punishments for disobedience are swift. Brutal. People disappear and no one questions it, because the word of the Judiciary is law."

"That's crazy," Maia protested, shaking her head. "I mean, after what they did to Ari we know they're bad, but what you're describing—"

"What I'm describing is fear. The Judiciary has ruled our people for centuries, and they do it through terror. They have us scared of ocean magic, scared of the humans, scared of the enforcers, and scared of some ancient monster."

"You're saying ocean magic isn't dangerous?" Dhanya countered. "That you don't think the Beast is a threat?"

Dhanya didn't look to Noah. Her dark eyes remained fastened on Willa and her voice gave nothing away.

"I'm saying that ocean magic is more complicated than we've been told," Willa replied, "but that the Judiciary's purposes are served by keeping that knowledge away from us. I'm saying that yes, the Beast is dangerous—beyond measure, dangerous—but that in exchange for supposed protection from that monster, our people have sacrificed more than they even understand. They let the Judiciary do all kinds of horrible things because of this, up to and including things like what they did to her."

Her sharp gaze went to me and I stopped breathing. She knew. She knew about what they'd done to me. Under the pillow, my arms started to sting all over again. My head moved of its own accord, a tiny shake.

Willa saw it. Harvey did too. His brow knitted, but Willa simply turned back to the others after only a heartbeat of a pause.

"Plenty of people within the resistance knew your father," she said to Jace. "He met with our operatives countless times. He kept the resistance informed of his brother's actions, of developments within the Judiciary, anything he learned."

"And we're just supposed to believe that?" Jace retorted.

Willa paused. "Harvey?"

"Miguel should really be the one—"

"Just tell them your part."

"Oh." The little man fidgeted with the edge of his tweed jacket. "Do you, uh, remember southern Utah, when you were…" He seemed to run a calculation in his head. "Eleven? Your father took you on a trip to Zion National Park."

Jace didn't appear to be breathing. "You could have heard about that any number of ways."

Harvey nodded nervously. "Well, yes, but on the way there, you stopped at a restaurant. A little place with red checkerboard tablecloths, James Dean posters, and a jukebox in the corner that played 'Love Me Tender' on a loop four times. He, um, he left you in the third booth from the door on the west side of the restaurant and spent twenty-three minutes talking to a man by the front counter—though she interrupted once because she wanted a root beer float for lunch." He nodded toward me.

Jace was pale.

"That was me, that day," Harvey continued. "He met with others too. There was the café where you all stopped on your way to the Grand Canyon, and that camping trip to Coconino

National Forest. The trip down Route 66 also provided several places that—"

"Enough," Jace said.

Harvey floundered. "We can help you. We've been searching for you for days. We knew you were traveling with—" He twitched his head toward Maia. "—so it made sense that, no matter how, um, *intact* Ariabella was after her, um, experience at the warehouse in Santa Lucina, you'd try to have Judge Davenport undo what was done to her."

My attention twitched across the others, but they were watching Harvey and didn't look at me.

Thankfully.

"We received other reports, though," Harvey continued, "of increased security around Judge Davenport's home, so there was a sixty-four percent probability that the Judiciary had anticipated your destination. We had to act fast. We stood the best chance of finding you by concentrating our efforts in a narrow band, rather than a broad sweep of terrain, and the odds were strongly in favor of you avoiding main roads, as well as traveling at night. I also calculated a seventy-one percent likelihood that you'd keep to places where you could use cash and park out of sight, which left motels of a certain construction type as the best choice, and the less visibly popular, the better. But the Judiciary may come to this conclusion as well. Based on the average rate of speed on northern California highways at this time of year, though, and factoring in construction as well as road hazards, there was a sixty—"

"We get it," Jace interrupted.

Harvey seemed to wilt under my brother's cold stare. "We drove around," he finished. "A lot. And we found her SUV behind the building."

"Why are you doing this?" Noah asked. "Charity because you knew her dad? How did you even hear about what happened to Ari?"

"We know because we have informants in all levels of ruanir society," Willa replied. "One of them was inside the Judiciary's Beast project. She was called in by the judges yesterday, last minute, to assist with the next steps of the procedure."

"You had someone there," Noah stated.

His words were flat, but I could feel the anger boiling in him like magma beneath the surface of the earth. It pushed at me and I tensed, fighting not to give any sign.

Noah's gaze flicked to me. With effort, he reined the fury back in.

"You could have helped her!" Jace snapped at Willa. "You could have stopped this!"

"We had a woman who was ordered by the judges to come in for work only minutes after they found Ariabella," Willa said. "A woman who knew almost nothing of what she was being asked to do till she arrived, and who wouldn't have had a *chance* of helping Ariabella, not against the enforcers and judges who were there. As it stood, our informant only managed to get short messages to us—enough for us to know a small measure of what the Judiciary planned, who they had, and where the lab was located. And we haven't learned anything since. We lost contact with her after the Beast attacked. We think that thing might've killed her."

Noah didn't move. Didn't even blink. But the anger in him became tinged with a wary sort of discomfort.

"We're helping because what they've done to your friend is sick and wrong," Willa continued. "Ariabella isn't the only one they've made into a lab rat over the years. Members of the resistance don't fare well when captured by the Judiciary."

She glanced around to the others. "We're taking a calculated risk, coming to you like this. We know about Jace and Ariabella's mother, Claudia Corvienne, and how she offered up her own daughter for experimentation. We know you had hardly any contact with her prior to Adam Moreau's death. And we're gambling that even with all your familial connections—" She looked pointedly to Maia and Dhanya. "—that you're not a blind supporter of the Judiciary. And that, since you ran from the judges rather than turn your cousins in, you also aren't interested in allowing them to continue whatever it is they've planned for Ariabella."

"But how can you help her?" Jace asked. "You got a judge on your payroll?"

Willa's cold expression didn't falter at his derisive tone. "Something like that."

Jace's eyes narrowed.

"What does that mean?" I asked, my heart pounding.

Willa's mouth tightened. "Like I said, ocean magic is complicated. Some of our people are working on ways to handle it again."

I froze and my family did the same.

"They *what?*" Dhanya demanded.

"Come with us and you'll see."

Dhanya was already shaking her head before Willa finished speaking. Maia glanced between her fiancée and the other girl, obvious reluctance on her face.

Jace had become a statue.

"Then what happens?" Baylie asked into the silence. "We're supposed to think you're just going to undo what they did and let Ari go? That you don't have some plan for using it too?"

Willa gave her a flat look.

"What about the Beast?" Baylie pressed. "The judges wanted to use her to control it. What are you after?"

"Not that," Willa said.

Baylie's expression hardened. Willa tossed a glance to Harvey.

"T-the Beast is a threat, yes," Harvey admitted, "and the events of the last week have forced numerous recalculations of its probable actions, but…" He swallowed hard, clearly trying to keep calm. "But we can stay safe from it. We have devices similar to what the judges have for tracking it. Our people cobbled them together from data and resources we stole from the Judiciary. We can't follow it in human form any more than the judges can, but in its natural state, its magical signature is large enough to be visible to our sensors. Before we lost it against the background noise of the deep ocean, we saw that it returned there. From all we can tell, it is still far underwater, recuperating. Additionally, we have an electrical field to—"

"No." The word left me before I could stop it.

Harvey blinked at me.

"No, you're not using some electrical weapon on—on it. The judges had something like that. What hurts the Beast hurts me. I'm not—"

"Oh, no, no," Harvey assured me hurriedly. "We've heard of those. This isn't the same. This is going to mask you and the rest of us. Right now, you're all in danger if it comes back and tries to find Ariabella, but the shield should keep it from locating you."

Noah was tense. Motionless in that way only he could do. I wished I could remind him to fake breathing or do anything else to keep them from suspecting he wasn't like us.

His attention twitched to me. I took a deep breath. His jaw muscles jumped, but he started breathing again.

"And if the Beast *does* come in contact with that field?" Noah asked carefully.

Harvey looked confused.

"Will that hurt it?" I pressed. "Hurt *me*?"

"It'd probably make it *uncomfortable*." Harvey fidgeted again, seeming uncomfortable himself. "It's not a defense shield, per se. We haven't really worked something like that out yet. Even what the judges have isn't really a defense; it's meant to drain the creature when they have it trapped. Ours is a signal-jamming device, similar to what our ancestors used in the early days, before they changed their magic enough that the creature couldn't find them." He shrugged helplessly. "But if the Beast can't feel that connection to you, there's no reason to assume it would—"

"What if it *did* get inside?" Baylie insisted.

"Well, I-I mean—"

"Then we would have bigger problems," Willa answered, "but we're prepared for that. We have evacuation routes, contingency plans. The facility is underground—an old bunker built in the Cold War days. Worst case, we have measures in place to collapse that on top of the Beast. It wouldn't kill it," she looked to me pointedly, "but it *would* slow it down for a time."

"We'll be safe," Harvey said. "Our reports show that the Beast is committed to self-preservation. We have a strong certainty of this based on its behavior over the past year and through historical records. Additionally, reports we've received from various informants indicate the Judiciary believes the dehaians are back in control of the creature. The fact that the dehaians haven't launched an all-out assault on us presents the possibility that they won't, that they'll be open to discussion. Additionally, because they and we are still alive, it would seem that the Beast hasn't retained its ability to operate independently and attack us on its own."

Nobody looked at Noah.

"We don't know why they woke the Beast again," Harvey continued. "Perhaps it was an accident. But warring over control of the creature will only end us up in the same position we were in centuries ago, battling the dehaians who, since they already control the thing, have the upper hand again."

Dhanya shook her head. "You haven't answered the question, though. Doesn't maintaining Ari's connection to the

Beast benefit you? Let you know where the Beast is? Maybe even control it, like the judges want to? Why should we believe you want to help her get rid of that, when you could clearly use it yourselves?"

Harvey looked to me. I tensed.

"We believe that is not the purpose of the connection," he allowed, appearing nervous at the words, "nor the intent for its use."

Jace scoffed. "What the hell is that supposed to mean?"

"The judges want the Beast dead," Willa said. "Of that much we're certain. Ariabella's connection to it was meant to draw the creature to them, into a trap, where they would kill the thing after harvesting magic from it. We have no such goal. We don't want its magic. We're not interested in whatever they planned to do with that magic either." Her blue eyes twitched to me and away again. I shivered. "We're not after a war with the dehaians—though if there's a chance for peace, we're going to take it. But attempting to kill the Beast or engaging that thing in a fight won't do that. We want to protect our people, not have them end up as victims of a sentient storm monster."

I wasn't able to stop myself from looking at Noah this time. We couldn't risk it. If these people found out about him, he might get hurt. We couldn't—

"It's the best chance we have to help Ari." Noah didn't look to me, keeping his focus on Jace and Baylie. "No matter what."

Jace nodded. Baylie appeared nauseated.

I dropped my gaze to my lap. The spikes felt like they were gone, though I worried there might be holes torn in the underside of the pillow now. Meanwhile, I didn't know what to say. These people had just shown up out of nowhere with wild stories of quasi-judges with complicated ocean magic and my father being some kind of resistance leader.

In a way, it wasn't that different than last time. Someone offering to help me. Fix my problem, if only I'd trust them. The judges had said the same thing.

This had been the result.

I wanted to run, but there was nowhere to go. Judge Davenport had always been a long shot. The six of us versus him and the enforcers. Even with Noah, there'd only ever been a tiny chance that it would go well. And if Harvey and Willa were right, even *more* enforcers would be there now.

Of course, the two of them could be lying.

Or I could be running out of time to fix what had happened to me and reclaim my life.

There wasn't much of a choice.

"Okay," I agreed. "Take us to this resistance."

5

LOGAN

Following the judge's orders translated into driving around for over a day, and I was already sick of it.

I didn't bother to try to hide my frustration while we pulled into the parking lot of the hundredth motel since I'd left Santa Lucina. Whether the three enforcers with me saw my irritation was irrelevant. They wouldn't express an opinion. After all, I was basically their master. They'd obey me no matter what mood I was in.

It was a bright spot in this otherwise tedious day. I could get used to being surrounded with things like them.

The car came to a stop outside the rundown entrance. A grimy glass door gave a narrow view of a white wall and a bulletin board plastered with brochures for boring local attractions. Nondescript doors lined the side of the building, stretching away from the road. Despite the mid-morning hour, the parking lot was pretty much empty of vehicles, including the silver SUV we were looking for.

But Ari might have been here and, just like every other

cockroach-infested dump I'd seen thus far, that meant we needed to check it out.

I climbed from the car. One of the enforcers followed while the other two remained by the black sedan. A cheap bell clanged overhead when I pushed the motel door open.

At the weathered front desk, a brunette girl turned toward the sound, a cell phone in her hand. I took in her appearance quickly. She couldn't have been more than eighteen. From what I could see on her phone screen, we'd interrupted her in the middle of a text, and most of it looked like the emoji-filled girl-gibberish I found so annoying. Her discount-shop quality clothes revealed a hint of large breasts—most likely the only *actually* interesting thing about her—while her black eyeliner was so thick, I was amazed she could still see. The textbook and closed notebook on the counter behind her both looked practically new, meaning she probably spent more time flirting with boys than studying at whatever hick school she went to.

I hid a smile. I knew exactly how to handle girls like this.

"Hi!" she called cheerily, quickly stuffing the phone beneath the desk. "May I help you?"

"We're looking for someone," said the enforcer beside me. Hans, I think he'd told me his name was. It fit. With his short shock of blond hair and arms that appeared to have been stuffed with bowling balls, he looked like he'd been born to act in a movie staged in Nazi Germany.

Hell, he was ruanir and he seemed near forty. He'd probably *been* in Nazi Germany.

"Are you with the police?" the girl asked.

"No, nothing like that." I stepped closer and put a smile on my face. I knew the effect I'd have on her. Panty-melting, some girl had once described my smile.

I wouldn't have any trouble getting this backwoods moron to tell me what I wanted.

The result of my maneuver was immediate. An answering smile, nervous and still fighting to be professional, tugged at her lip.

"We're looking for my sister. Can you help us—" I glanced to her name tag. "Kelli?"

She started to shrug. "I'm sorry, I can't tell you—"

"It's important," I urged, meeting her boring brown eyes with an expression like she was the most vital person in the world to me.

The girl appeared flustered. Her eyes darted to Hans.

"This is my uncle George," I added. "He's helping me because he's super worried about—" I snagged a name out of a mental hat. "—Julia too."

Kelli tried another shrug. "I really can't—"

"They were driving a silver SUV," I pressed on, repeating what the enforcers had told me after we left Santa Lucina. "There would have been four or five of them. Three girls. One or two guys, one of which might have been blond."

She hesitated, but I could read it in her eyes. She'd seen something. There'd been a flash of recognition when I'd mentioned the SUV.

"You've seen her, haven't you? When? Where did she go?"

Kelli flushed and her weight shifted, almost like she wanted to retreat a step. "I didn't say that. I—"

"It's really important."

"Have you tried calling the police?"

"They won't do anything." I poured desperation into my voice. "It hasn't been forty-eight hours, right? You have to wait to report somebody missing. But it's not really like that. Julia's just sick and I need to know that she's safe. Was she here?"

A vein in Kelli's neck began twitching faster. Yet she glanced to the enforcer again, those damn debates continuing to rage, weighing whether to tell me anything.

She wasn't supposed to *think* this much.

"What about calling her? You could—"

"She isn't answering her phone." I exhaled, fighting off a surge of irritation. I enjoyed a challenge as much as the next guy, but Ari could be getting farther away by the second. I didn't have time for this. "Listen, I'm not asking you to break any laws. I only need to know if Julia was here and where she went. That's all."

"Well, it's just that there *are* laws about this sort of thing," Kelli hedged. "And my boss's policy is *really* strict…"

The image of reaching across the counter and strangling her flitted through my mind, clear as day. I poured the energy of it into a pleading expression instead.

"Please," I implored. "She needs her medication. If she doesn't get it…" I let my voice trail off, leaving the dire implications to hang in the air.

Kelli bit her lip, clearly torn. With a beseeching expression, I sent my gaze roaming over every mundane line of her face, even as I imagined pounding that face into the countertop. My poor, sick sister's life was at stake. Silence might get dear "Julia" hurt.

"There *was* a silver SUV," the infuriating girl admitted. "But it left already. I don't know if it was the one you want. I'm sorry, that's all I can tell y—"

The front door opened, the bell above it clanging loudly. Kelli flinched, alarm flashing over her face. I glanced back. A wiry man with a long, stringy ponytail walked into the room, pushing a plastic garbage bin on wheels ahead of him.

"I'm sorry," Kelli said. I turned to find her nervously fidgeting. "I really can't say more than that. Maybe the police will help you when you explain she's sick."

I didn't move. This little, backwoods bitch…

"My sister is going to die because of you," I stated flatly.

I stalked out the door. Hans followed and stopped behind me when I came to a halt several yards from the building.

It was all I could do not to go back in there.

"Orders, sir?" the enforcer said quietly.

A shiver ran through me at the words, and it calmed my rage. Sir. I liked that. And it was true. I was still in charge here.

God, I hated the stubborn ones. At least, the stubborn ones who I didn't have time to set up and watch fall apart, or simply deal with in a more direct manner. They were like malfunctioning toys, and about as entertaining.

I wondered if I could send the enforcers back in there once the maintenance man was gone. Have them get information out of her *their* way.

The thought was tempting.

I let out a breath. Tempting, but too risky. Even if they didn't use magic, between our fingerprints in the place, the man who'd remember our presence, and the security cameras in the corners, there were still too many chances for something to go wrong. And she wasn't worth it anyway. I had more important things to focus on. Ari had been here. Maybe, in any case. Some of the other staff in this pathetic little dump might—

The door clanged behind me. I glanced over my shoulder to find the maintenance guy wheeling the garbage can out of the front office. When he saw me look his way, he twitched his head toward the corner of the building before continuing onward, pushing the garbage bin in the same direction he'd indicated.

My eyes narrowed. With a brief check to the grimy front window of the main office, I trailed him around the corner, Hans at my heels.

The wiry man had stopped beyond the turn of the building. He cast a cagey glance around when we joined him. "You looking for somebody?"

"Yeah." I studied him. His thin hair had been collected into a ponytail and his clothes were clean enough to argue that he washed them frequently. He was interested in keeping his job, then. His teeth and his fingers were stained from cigarettes, though, and he smelled faintly of tobacco. Nicotine addict, probably with other addictions, if the way his hands shook was any indication. His bearing and constantly scanning eyes made it seem like he was used to back-alley dealings as well.

This might be more like it.

"My sister. She's about seventeen. Golden brown hair. Traveling with a group of four or five people in a silver SUV."

"I might've seen 'em."

I waited.

His gaze twitched toward my pocket and then away.

"Uncle George," I snapped to Hans.

The enforcer took out a hundred-dollar bill. The maintenance man's eyes widened for less than a heartbeat. Swiftly, he squirrelled the money away.

"Silver SUV showed up this morning before dawn. Six people in it, though. Four girls and two guys. One of the girls looked like she might be your sister. She didn't seem in great shape. A blond guy held onto her like she was gonna fall apart from walking."

That had to be the Beast, which meant Judge Engle's assertion might be true. That thing actually thought it *cared* about Ari. Meanwhile, she clearly wasn't doing well.

I wondered how screwed up she really might be.

"Did you see where they went?" I asked.

His gaze twitched again. Hans materialized another hundred from his wallet. It vanished into the maintenance man's grasp.

"They didn't stay long. A redheaded girl and an old, balding guy showed up shortly after. Didn't seem welcome at first. The redhead tried kicking the door down before they let her in. But then they all left together, the six of them in the SUV and the other two in a brown truck. Took off at about sunrise and drove east toward the highway."

I paused. Subversive forces, Judge Engle had said. The Judiciary already knew that Maia Davenport and Dhanya Singh had betrayed them. It was Maia's SUV they'd been tracking after all, and we'd been going north because the judges assumed Ari and the others would head for Maia's father.

But clearly those two weren't the only problem.

"Anything else?" I asked the man.

He hesitated, his eyes running fast across Hans. I could see him weighing the benefits of lying.

The sheer enormity of the enforcer behind me won out.

"No."

I nodded. Without another word, I headed for the sedan. "Get in the car," I called to the enforcers there.

They didn't move, their focus on Hans. I tossed a quick look back.

The man had stopped. "We must call the Judiciary," he said in a low voice.

"Excuse me?"

"We must inform them of this development."

"Why? We don't know where Ari is yet."

The man stared at me like a statue, waiting for me to do what he said.

I scoffed. I couldn't believe this. *I* was in charge here.

Okay, mostly in charge. I wasn't irrational. I knew the judges were the primary authority, at least for the time being. But Hans should still listen to me. He was an enforcer. He obeyed the Judiciary and anyone who spoke for it.

In other words, me.

"We don't know where she is," I reiterated. "They've got at least a five-hour lead on us and they could have gone anywhere on that highway, *if* they even got on it at all. You're insisting I waste the Judiciary's time when we've discovered next to nothing. The judges won't be happy with that."

"But we have information about a direction."

"And that's all we have. We're in California, Hans; the whole *country* is east of here. We need more specifics before we just call the judges up."

"There are only four of us. Should we encounter the Beast during our investigation, we will require reinforcements if we wish to survive."

I paused. There was that.

Turning away from him, I pulled out my phone.

Judge Engle picked up after only one ring. "Report."

"I have a lead." I filled him in on the details the maintenance man had given me.

Judge Engle paused. "A redhead and a balding man."

He said that like he knew them. "Yes, sir."

I heard quiet voices in the background, their words unintelligible.

"Head for Dawson Hill Bed and Breakfast."

"Sir?"

"We've received word of a possible hideout location for the subversive forces about whom I told you. This information may confirm its existence. The redhead in question sounds like Willa Blackwood. The Judiciary has suspected her of harboring seditionist sympathies for some time. We will send a dozen more enforcers to assist you, and they will meet you at the highway rest area twenty miles east of your destination. Hans will know the specifics of the location. Call us once the enforcers have completed the rest of their task with Miss Moreau."

The line went dead.

I lowered the phone, blinking at the rapid-fire barrage of orders. Willa Blackwood. I remembered her. Daughter of some Judiciary lackey or other, with a model's body and a face to match. I'd intended to hook up with her a few years back, to see if that athletic build translated into other skills I suspected she had.

But then she'd vanished. Something about her parents, maybe. The details hadn't been important at the time.

And now she was here. Meeting with traitors. Rebelling against the Judiciary. Hiding Ari.

Quite possibly hiding the Beast.

My gaze slid back toward Hans. For a moment, I studied him, imagining the magical poison that I knew lurked beneath his skin.

Anticipation tingled through me. "Let's go."

The man didn't waste a second in moving toward the sedan. The other enforcers climbed in quickly, not questioning the order at all.

I kept from chuckling to myself. Now *that* was more like it.

6

NOAH

There had to be a word for continuing on when you had no options. For knowing that the choice in front of you was almost certainly bad but having no other alternative.

Trapped. The word was probably trapped.

I fought off a scowl while I watched the road through a window of the SUV. Ari and I had stayed on the fold-down seats in the back, while the others had taken the regular seats ahead of us. In the time since we left the motel, no one had said a word, barring a quick phone call Baylie received from Diane, my stepmother. She'd wanted Baylie to know the dehaians had been warned. Chloe and Zeke sent word, thanking her. From the sound of it, they hadn't mentioned anything about me to my stepmother.

Neither had Baylie.

I shifted on the seat. I couldn't worry about that right now. My dad or Diane. My brother. It hurt and sucked and I didn't know what to do about it—I hadn't known for a year—but they were safe. That was the important thing.

It was the rest of us I was worried about. Ari needed help, yes, but for these people to show up out of nowhere with stories about some ruanir resistance, who inexplicably wanted to fix this… it seemed hard to believe.

And *way* too much like it might be a setup.

That was the problem, though. If this was a setup, it still meant the judges had known where we were headed. Or that someone *else* was after Ari—someone else who wanted to use her.

Yet there wasn't a choice. There just wasn't. The incredibly slim chance this *wasn't* a trap was our only hope, and we needed help. At least with this supposed "resistance" there was a possibility of changing what had happened to Ari.

What *was* happening.

My shoulders twitched with discomfort. Stages, the judges had said. The judges planned more for her than what they'd already done, so whatever this was, it wasn't over yet.

Ari fidgeted next to me, a strange echo of my own uneasiness coming from her, along with a hint of questioning. She hadn't missed what I was feeling. There wasn't much chance she could.

I reached over and wrapped my fingers around hers, trying not to let on that touching her worried me. My magic catalyzed what they'd changed in her. Part of it, anyway. We might be okay with simply holding hands, but I still had to be careful. I didn't want to accidentally let slip any of the energy twisting inside me.

In any case, touching her made it hard to think lately. Ever since that night when she fell asleep next to me on the porch at Baylie's, or since I'd held her while she cried underwater, or since she'd changed form and my hands had ended up on nothing but her soft, naked body…

I gritted my teeth, fighting to obliterate the disconcerting memories. I didn't need this. I couldn't think like this. Having someone in my head all the time… it was messing with me.

Ari's hand tightened on mine and confused worry came at me. My frustration grew. This wasn't helping either of us. I needed to think about something else. *Anything* else.

Up ahead, Willa and Harvey's rust-eaten truck turned, leaving the country highway we'd been following for God knew how long. Jace sent the SUV after it. Several minutes later, we were driving down a dirt track, the late morning sun making the landscape glow. The highway was long since out of sight. I could feel the ocean getting stronger in the air, though. We were closer to the sea than we'd been since leaving Santa Lucina, close enough that I expected to see it on the horizon past the hills at any moment. The truck bounced over potholes and rocks ahead of us, sending up a cloud of dust in its wake. No other cars seemed to be on the road at this hour, and even though we were near the ocean, on this patch of coast the houses were still few and far between.

Willa slowed. I caught sight of a wooden sign on our right, its surface painted white with blue letters that told us the Dawson Hill Bed and Breakfast lay down the road. A hand-drawn arrow below the words directed us to turn ahead.

She did. We followed.

The air began to feel strange, almost as if it was humming with electricity.

I looked to the windows again. I remembered this sensation. I'd felt it a lifetime ago on the Oregon coast. It wasn't quite the same, though. Similar, yet not the same, and it sent alarm spiking through me.

I scanned the ragged landscape. Not far from the edge of the road, a metal utility box peeked above the grass. Another stood on the opposite side, and another still farther into the field. I caught a glimpse of symbols etched on their sides, though the details were hard to make out over the distance.

But it was the defense against the Beast. It had to be. Stone pillars or metal utility boxes, the effect was the same as it had been last year at Joseph's hideout. Nauseating. Chilling. My body had already started shaking. The ruanir in the car weren't reacting, though, and I knew it wouldn't affect humans. But me, Ari…

In the passenger seat, Baylie made an uncomfortable noise. I looked to her in alarm.

"You okay?" Jace asked her.

She hesitated. "Yeah, just carsick."

I winced. She had to be picking up on this from me.

Ari's hand tightened on mine, pulling my attention away. I could feel her trembling. "Noah…" she whispered.

A hint of green glistened in her skin.

"Just hang on." I was beginning to feel like someone was sawing barbed wire through my insides. "It'll be over in a second."

She looked confused.

"Their defense against the Beast," I managed. "Joseph had something similar."

At the name of the old, turtle-like wizard, her confusion cleared. "To keep you out."

I gave a short nod. I'd broken through something like this a year ago—the Beast part of me had, anyway—and while that barrier had been weakened by Chloe's magic, this one wasn't as strong to begin with. Joseph had been dealing with huge amounts of ocean magic and trying to hide it from the Beast. These people were only trying to hide Ari, not enough power to blow up a city.

A shudder ran through me. The Beast had enjoyed that day, even if the rest of me hadn't.

The vehicles crested a rise. The barbed wire sensation began to dissipate. Ari let out a breath, her skin returning to normal. Her gaze darted over the others, checking if any of them had noticed.

No one had, at least not that I could tell. I looked to Baylie. Her head in her hands, she still seemed to be fighting off nausea.

"Baylie?" I called.

"I'm fine," she replied without turning around.

I watched her, concerned, but after a moment she took a breath and straightened like nothing had happened.

I kept an eye on her for a second longer and then glanced to the road. A sprawling, Craftsman-style mansion waited ahead. The two-story place was a brownish shade of green, while the shingles on the pointed roof were black. A roughhewn stone overlay covered the walls on the lower half of the first floor, while large wooden pillars surrounded by flowering plants supported the wide porch. The windows were arched, and the treated glass kept anyone from being able to see inside, affording them a reflection of the landscape instead.

It didn't exactly look like the Cold War bunker Willa had described.

Ahead of us, Willa steered the truck onto a cobblestone drive leading to the house. Jace pulled up behind her when she came to a stop.

I checked around as we left the SUV. I could feel the ocean not far from here, though the countryside was quiet, with only bird calls and the sound of the wind in the grass. The house itself was still. No one came outside. I couldn't see anything beyond those treated windows.

I missed my greliaran hearing. Time was, I could've picked up on anything for a mile around in a quiet place like this. Similarly, taking off and getting a bird's-eye view of our surroundings would've been nice, but the judges could track me in my other form and they'd simply know right where we were again.

If they didn't already.

The door to the house opened. I tensed.

An older woman walked out onto the porch. She was tall and slender with a bearing like a queen. She wore a chocolate-brown pantsuit with gold jewelry and her gray hair was done up in a style that reminded me of pictures of actresses from the 1930s. Her hand resting lightly on the porch banister, she descended the steps toward us.

"Wilhelmina," she said. "I didn't realize you needed to be a part of this outing today."

Jaw muscles jumping, Willa didn't respond for a moment. "Grandmother," she replied coldly. "Is Miguel here?"

Her grandmother's red lips thinned. "Yes. He is downstairs confirming that you were not followed."

"Great." Willa looked to Harvey. "Meet you there?"

Without waiting for his response, she strode toward the steps. The old woman's displeased expression deepened.

Willa seemed to ignore it.

Her grandmother turned back to us while Willa disappeared inside. "Mister Stolberg, how nice to see you again."

Harvey tried for a smile. "Sorry. I couldn't really tell her not to—"

"Oh, no one could do that, believe me. I see you have guests."

Harvey bobbed his head. "Ariabella and Jace Moreau, and their, um… well, some of them are family and I'm not really sure about—"

"How lovely to meet you all," the woman said smoothly over his nervous words. "I am Fiona Blackwood. Won't you come inside?"

She turned, climbing the steps to the broad porch again.

I looked to Ari. She was a bundle of nerves, but I had the weirdest feeling that what scared her wasn't necessarily… here, somehow. It didn't make sense.

"You okay?" I whispered.

She glanced to me and her lip twitched up in an anxious smile. "Y-yeah." She started toward the house. Watching her carefully, I followed.

Wood dominated the interior of the mansion, all of it polished and gleaming. Oak beams stretched across the high ceiling of the parlor to our right and above the corridor ahead. Stone surrounded the large fireplace in the sitting room; the rocks matched the ones decorating the house's exterior. Sunlight streamed through the windows, warming the couches and chairs scattered throughout the room. Stationed in the corridor and the parlor, a half dozen repairmen ostensibly fixed lights on the ceiling or rewired switches on the wall. They looked over when we came in, regarding us with flat, assessing stares that instantly set me on edge.

Bodyguards. They had to be. I couldn't see their weapons but given how their hands continually hovered near the insides of their toolboxes, I had to believe their guns weren't far away.

Fiona ignored them and gestured to the chairs. "Please sit down. May I get anyone something to drink? Coffee, perhaps?"

"What is this?" Jace demanded in a low voice. He cast a short glance to the workmen. "We came here for someone to help my sister, not to have morning coffee."

Fiona smiled. "Of course, but as I told my granddaughter, the others are confirming that you were not followed. I'm certain you can understand our need for caution."

Maia glanced to the windows while Jace glowered. Warily, I sank onto the couch with Ari by my side.

Fiona's smile never wavered. "So tell me, where are you all

most recently from?"

Curiosity flickered through me at the strange phrasing of the question.

"Chicago," Dhanya replied. "Our parents have been there for several decades."

"Indeed?" Fiona sounded pleasantly surprised. "I lived in Chicago in the nineteen-twenties. Such an interesting city. Do you find it enjoyable now?"

Dhanya smiled. "We do, yes."

I looked back to the windows, trying not to show any reaction. The ruanir were virtually immortal compared to humans. Once they went through their "adjustment" at roughly around eighteen or so, they gradually began to age one year or less for every four.

It was disconcerting to be reminded of it so casually.

A buzzing broke the quiet. Fiona lifted a cell phone from an end table nearby and regarded the screen briefly. "Ah, that was Miguel. It appears all is well." She rose to her feet again. "If you would come this way?"

She walked toward the hall.

I looked over when Ari didn't move.

Ari blinked and then gave me a nervous smile. "Feels like when the judges took me down to connect me to, you know, the Beast. Except..." She glanced around, her discomfort growing. "Well, I guess you all might've been there then too."

She swallowed hard and pushed to her feet, hurrying toward Fiona. I strode after her.

The workmen's eyes tracked us the entire way.

Fiona passed through a door off the side of the long, wood-paneled corridor and then paused at the far end of a small library beyond. She reached up, taking the top of one leather-covered book among countless others, and pulled it partially from the shelf.

A click followed. The bookcase swung back like a secret passageway in a movie.

Which, more or less, was precisely what it was.

A stairwell waited behind it. Walls of concrete surrounded the spiraling steps. Utility lights flickered to life above them.

Fiona stepped aside. "Mister Stolberg, if you wouldn't mind leading the rest of the way?"

Harvey nodded quickly and started down the stairs.

Ari let out a breath as if steadying herself. Jace took one look at her and then moved to go first.

"Again, it's been a pleasure to meet you all," Fiona said.

I wondered if she meant the words to sound so final.

And if so, why.

We trailed Harvey through the doorway. Fiona closed the bookcase behind us.

I paused, feeling a bit like we were being sealed into a trap.

"It's okay," Harvey offered nervously. I looked down the stairway to see that he'd noticed my hesitation. "Fiona… well, she hates underground spaces. I know that might seem odd, given that she owns this place. She had it built for the rest of us back in the sixties when nuclear war paranoia meant no one would ask too many questions about the whole undertaking. But she was also caught in one of the last witch hunts of the seventeen hundreds. The villagers tried to bury her alive."

I faltered, shocked, and Baylie's expression clearly showed she was too. The others kept moving, though, showing little response to Harvey's explanation besides sympathy. Apparently, stories like that were normal to them—a fact which in itself felt surreal.

I started walking again. Our footsteps on the metal stairs became the only sound on a descent that never seemed to end. I eyed the area around us, wondering how deep we were.

And what it would feel like to have this much rock drop on me if something went wrong and these people figured out what I was. I probably wouldn't die. I could affect the ground a bit—cause shallow earthquakes and the like, even though it took a tremendous amount of effort—so I'd be able to get out of this eventually. But Willa was still right. It would damn well slow me down.

It did raise the question of what would happen to *Ari* if they dropped this on me, though…

Worry emanated from Ari, directed at me. She could tell something was upsetting me.

I shoved the thoughts down hard, struggling to keep calm and not think about it for her sake. I'd protect her, that's what would happen. I'd get her out of here at the first sign these people weren't who they claimed.

The base of the stairway came into view. A metal door waited there, covered in bolts and braces. It looked strong enough to withstand a cannon. A small keypad was affixed to the wall beside it. Quickly, Harvey tapped in a series of numbers.

A clunking noise came from the door. Harvey took hold of the thick handle and pulled it back.

The door opened and with it came a wall of sound. Clanks. Hisses of steam. People talking. Calling to each other.

Harvey walked inside. We followed him into a room large enough to be a warehouse, despite the fact it was underground. Concrete defined its appearance, from the gray walls and floor all the way up to the distant ceiling. Yellow paint sectioned off various spaces on the ground in bright, harsh lines. An enormous steel machine stood at the center, like a distillery on steroids. Glass canisters were positioned around it, each of them taller than a person and wide enough that three people could stand around them with their arms out and their hands wouldn't even touch. Clear liquid bubbled inside. Thick pipes ran from the canisters to the machine, and from the machine into the ceiling and walls. Computer stations circled it all, their screens showing bar graphs and ticking lines I could only assume were monitoring systems of some kind. Glass panels hung on the walls. Maps were etched on them and blushes of color glowed on their surface.

I tensed. That was how the judges tried to track me, though my human form had hidden me from their devices. No one here was shouting or pointing, though. Hopefully Harvey and Willa were right, and these people really did have the same problem.

Ari's hand found mine. I glanced over to see her eyes on the glass panes too.

From among the people watching the glass panels and the

computers, a man walked toward us. Latino with a medium build, he appeared to be about forty, though for a ruanir that could mean almost anything. He wore a dark canvas jacket and gray cargo pants that had the look of military issue.

Jace stopped. "Uncle *Mike?*"

The corner of the guy's mouth lifted. "Hey, Jace. Long time, no see."

I glanced between them. Ari had never mentioned an uncle other than the one who was a judge. Maia and Dhanya looked confused as well, as if this were also news to them.

"I'd ask how you've been, but…"

Jace nodded slowly. "Yeah."

The guy smiled. He moved as if to extend a hand toward me. "Hello."

Ari stepped between us. "You're the man who can help me?"

His gaze flashed between me and Ari so fast, it was barely more than a blink of his eye. But he'd caught how she'd blocked him from touching me. I was sure of it.

"Yeah," he said, extending the hand to her as if that'd been his goal the entire time. "It's good to see you as well, Ari. My name's Miguel Salazar."

She shook his hand warily.

"He knew Dad," Jace explained. "Came over a lot when we were kids."

Miguel nodded. "Your father was my primary contact in the judges' world before he defected from their ranks of initiates. Which was always the plan, by the way. He held in there as long as he could before they stopped allowing him to postpone their treatments."

"Okay," Ari said. "Well, um…"

"We know you, Ari," Miguel assured her, "and we know what happened."

Tension spiked higher in Ari. She moved as if to retreat from him and her hand found mine again.

Curiosity flew through the man's eyes.

"Where've you been?" Jace asked. "We haven't seen you in—"

"Since before your dad died," Miguel picked up as if he hadn't noticed anything. "We cut off contact to try to keep you all safe. Guess the judges had other ideas."

He glanced back as another man came toward us. Dark-haired, pale, and thin like his body had been stretched too far, he wore a white lab coat over his black shirt and pants. A contemptuous look hovered on his face, as if Ari and the rest of us were children who had stumbled into a grownup's world.

I disliked him immediately.

"They said you can feel the presence of the Beast?" the guy snapped at Ari without preamble.

Ari blinked. "I, um…" She looked to Miguel.

"Everyone," Miguel stepped in. "This is Declan Kane, head of what we call the Breakmire Initiative. Ocean magic project. Declan, this is Ari Moreau, her brother Jace, and—"

Declan made an impatient noise. "Yeah, yeah. Ari's boyfriend and some other girls to get in my way. Great. Whatever."

Mortification shot through Ari. She dropped her hand from mine like it burned. "He's not my—"

"Can you tell where the Beast is?" Declan interrupted.

"Declan," Miguel said.

The guy didn't look away from Ari.

"A-a bit," she allowed. "Sometimes."

Declan swore and started toward the machines.

Ari took a step after him. "But—"

"But?" Declan turned back. "But *what?*"

"I mean, not *now.* Just in general. A bit in general. Those things outside. The, um—"

"The *shielding anchors?*"

Anger surged inside me at Declan's scathing tone. Who the hell did this guy think he—

"Yes." Ari's hand twitched toward me as if to calm me down, and then embarrassment stilled the motion. "They stopped it. I can't tell anything about… about the Beast anymore."

She didn't look away from him at the lie.

Declan smirked, glancing to Miguel. "Told you it'd work."

Miguel ignored him. "But you can normally?" he asked Ari.

She floundered. I resisted the urge to reach out to her this time.

"Harvey and Willa said you'd pick up on it if it left the ocean," Baylie cut in. "Wouldn't you know?"

Relief shot through Ari. I could've hugged Baylie.

"*Unless* it's in human form," Declan retorted. "Then, no. That freak of nature's wearing the shape like camouflage. Drops off our sensors when it's like that, so we can't find it. Can you?"

He directed the question to Ari, his tone accusatory.

She shifted her weight uncomfortably. "Please just fix

whatever this is, okay?"

"If that creature comes for you—"

"Then we'll evacuate and you'll bring the whole place down on it," Miguel said. "Fiona's watching for any visitors besides our friends here, we have plenty of tricks up our sleeves, and if we get so much as a *hint* that thing is nearby, you'll get to use them. It'll be fine."

Declan scowled.

Miguel turned back to Ari. "Can you find it in human form?"

She shook her head.

"Have you *seen* it in human form?"

Ari hesitated. "No."

"It was at that warehouse," Declan snapped. "It blew the whole building up. You're telling us it didn't appear in human form at *any* point?"

"No," Ari repeated, more emphatically. "I didn't see it."

"Fine," Miguel interjected before Declan could start in again.

"Willa told us you could help me," Ari said. "That you have some kind of ocean magic that your people use—"

"It's more complicated than that," Declan sniped.

"How?" Baylie retorted. Nearly as tense as Ari, she seemed unable to keep her eyes from twitching to the scientists around us.

"It's not something we can just *explain,*" Declan said. "It takes years to—"

"Yes," Miguel cut in. "We do. And yes, we will use it to help you."

Another exasperated noise left Declan. He turned around and strode toward the machines.

"I'm sorry," Miguel said, irritation coloring his tone. "But just so you know, Declan's not an example of what happens from our form of ocean magic. He can even manage to be civil on rare occasions. But the Breakmire Initiative is all he has left, thanks to the judges. Fifteen years ago, he was an up-and-coming scientist for the Judiciary, on the fast track to be the main researcher for their premier projects. But when he started asking too many questions, the bastards tried to destroy him. They wiped out his career with reports of falsified data, scandals, you name it. They burned his home and left evidence pointing to him as proof of his 'madness'. They even killed his wife and daughter. This project is his revenge, and he takes every piece of it about as personally as you could possibly imagine. Try to ignore his outbursts, if you can."

The others around me nodded.

"Is it really safe, though?" Maia asked. "This ocean magic? You don't end up poisoned like the people who—"

"You really believe all those people poisoned themselves?"

Maia's face became a picture of alarm. Something colder and more sickened came from Ari.

"What does that mean?" Dhanya asked, that clinical edge creeping into her voice. I was beginning to suspect the analytical tone was a defense mechanism, especially given the fear I could see in her dark eyes.

Her grandmother died of "ocean magic poisoning", I

remembered. Oh hell.

"Our people live in terror of an outbreak," Miguel said, "and yet every couple of years, someone crops up with exactly that problem. How could *so* many ruanir continually be so foolish?" His gaze skimmed across us all. "You never wondered about that."

No one responded.

"The judges make anyone who challenges them disappear," Miguel continued. "All they have to say is 'ocean magic', and everyone ceases to question. After all, those who *do* return—who manage to 'survive their exposure'—are never the same, which makes the supposed danger more than clear."

"So… what?" Dhanya pressed. "You're saying ocean magic isn't toxic?"

"I'm saying it's convenient, that poisoning claim. Ocean magic *is* toxic to us—there isn't one of us who could handle it the way our ancestors did. Chances are, there never will be. And the judges *were* helpful in protecting us against it… once. But now—" He scoffed. "Now it's a great excuse.

"When someone is taken away, it's almost never because they've been poisoned. It's often because they're one of *our* people. A rebel, or even just a ruanir who's started to question the Judiciary's rule. Someone who's started to wonder if there's another way. Sometimes the supposed victim of poisoning is even one of their friends or family members being used as leverage. But when the judges are done, that same person is now simply another poster child for why the Judiciary is so necessary. Why the ocean is so dangerous." He glanced to Ari.

"And they're usually too damaged by the so-called treatments to argue with the depiction."

Fear and nausea rolled through Ari. She wanted to run.

"Why would they do that?" Dhanya insisted, her clinical tone shakier than before.

"To maintain power," Miguel replied. "Our ancestors made a monster, Miss Singh. One every bit as terrible as the Beast. They made leaders with no conscience and no empathy. They thought impartiality was so important that they sacrificed everything else, including any check on that power. They gave them the perfect control measure as well—a fear of ocean magic. A boogeyman against which only *they* could supposedly defend. You think they want to lose that kind of authority?"

Dhanya didn't say a word.

"But you've found a way to handle that magic?" Ari asked, her voice tight.

Miguel's lip rose in a dry smile. "Declan," he called.

"What?" the other man snapped from across the room.

"Demonstration."

Declan looked incredulous. "Are you kidding? I was waiting till we were ready for the tests on the Moreau girl. I'll need time to recover."

Miguel regarded him silently.

Declan's annoyance grew at whatever he saw in the man's expression. "*Fine.*" He stalked toward the machine towering over the center of the room.

"This way," Miguel said.

Cautiously, we followed him. I eyed the machine. Joseph

had had something similar at his house on the coast, only this thing was a whole lot larger. The old man had intended his machine to distill magic from the water too, though in that case the goal had been reclaiming traces of the old energy from before the dehaians had changed themselves to hide from the Beast.

But that energy was back again. I was proof of it. So there shouldn't have been a need for an operation of this magnitude to distill *that* from the water, especially this close to the sea.

Declan climbed a ladder on the side of one of the glass canisters of the machine. At the top, he reached over, pulled a lever, and then winched open the lid.

Something strange filtered into the air. It wasn't quite ocean magic—at least, not the kind I was used to. It felt like a surface I'd touched a thousand times had suddenly changed. Like an unexpected scent in familiar air. Like food missing one necessary ingredient.

I couldn't stop myself from recoiling. This wasn't like what Joseph had done. This wasn't like anything I'd ever experienced.

"You're safe," Miguel assured me. "Like I said, ocean magic *is* dangerous—but only without proper protection and filtration. Which is exactly what this is. Our ancestors used to be able to handle this on their own, but by altering ourselves to avoid the Beast, we essentially made ourselves allergic to that energy. So we've brought in ocean water and distilled down the magic within it, rendering a form that won't hurt us. These canisters contain the final stages. Mere air exposure isn't enough to harm anyone, not over the short period of time we'll need here."

I didn't respond, glancing to Ari. She had a nauseated look on her face. Beyond her, Baylie did as well.

I tried not to frown. Ari was one thing, but if Baylie was sickened by this too, it meant my own reaction had to be carrying through to them both.

Not that there was much I could do about it, besides fight to keep myself from absorbing even a shred of *whatever* the hell that actually was.

"So he…" Maia began.

"Is our version of a judge, yes. Declan, several others, even my wife, Veronique. They've been studying how to do this for years, trying to perfect the process, and in the past few months, they've finally figured out a way. We think it has something to do with the Beast's return, some alteration of the magic from the ocean that has brought the energy closer to what it used to be. And now…"

"What do you want?" Declan asked Miguel waspishly.

"Charge the road stations to the west, where they came through."

Declan looked disgusted. "Just to show off for the kiddies? Miguel, I set those up myself. This isn't—"

"Humor me."

The words were simple, but they held a tone of command that made Declan pause.

"Fine." Declan glanced around to the other people near the machines. "Charging Grid Delta."

He extended one hand over the bubbling liquid and held the other toward the ceiling.

The uncomfortable feeling in the air grew… concentrated. More ahead of me than behind, as if it was being pulled toward something now. And then it shifted, like a slow drain of water suddenly transforming into a raging firehose. Magic surged upward from Declan's hand.

It was all I could do not to stumble back. The invisible flood slammed into the ceiling, rushed over it, and electricity sparked from tiny metal bars that I hadn't noticed protruding from the concrete there. Like metal filings drawn to a magnet, the charge localized on a trio of those poles. The bars flared to life like sticks in a fire, though only a moment passed before the magic seemed to absorb into them and they lost their glow.

The strange feeling in the air faded back to the way it had been a short time before. I shuddered, glancing down in spite of myself to make sure shock and nausea hadn't drained my skin of more color than was naturally possible. The last thing I needed was these people seeing me turn gray.

At my side, Ari fumbled her hand into mine. I could feel her shaking.

"Grid Delta fully charged," called a woman by one of the computers.

On the ladder, Declan sagged against the side of the canister and muttered something heated.

Miguel ignored him. "Ocean magic—a new form of it. Perfectly safe, possessing none of the side effects the judges have threatened us with over the years."

"No side effects," Declan added. "Except that it's *exhausting*, so it shouldn't be used *wastefully*."

He slammed the lid shut. The nauseating magic drained from the air. I barely kept from closing my eyes with sheer relief.

Miguel glanced up to Declan. The scrawny man's face tightened, but he didn't say anything more as he started down from the ladder.

"This is what we'll use to help you," Miguel said to Ari. "And this is why we hope we *can* help you. The mess hall should serve as a decent waiting area till we're ready. Once Declan recovers—" He nodded toward the glowering man. "—he and several others will examine what was done to you. Jace, you and the others can stay in the mess hall if you'd like, or—"

"No, we're going with her," Jace cut in.

"Or you can watch from the observation area," Miguel continued smoothly. "Either option is good with us."

Jace nodded.

"Um…" Harvey started.

"Stay with them till we're ready and then meet Willa back in the surveillance room. Work with her to learn what you can of Shannon's whereabouts."

Harvey nodded quickly.

"It was good to see you again," Miguel said, directing the words to Ari and Jace. "Both of you." He gave us a final smile and then headed for an exit on the far side of the room.

"Shannon?" Maia asked.

Harvey fidgeted with the bottom of his jacket. "Our informant from the Beast project."

He fled the room through the nearest door. The others

hesitated, and then trailed after him.

Ari's eyes met mine nervously. I didn't know what to feel or what to make of everything we'd been told. Complicated wasn't even the half of it. Everything to do with the ruanir just kept getting crazier, as if every day, each new thing we survived only proved to be a dress rehearsal for more insanity.

Except this time, it might help her. This time, we might finally start making some headway against those judge bastards and their plans.

If she could withstand whatever the hell that magic was.

I scowled. She would. Or I'd get her out of here. But meanwhile, there was this Shannon woman to worry about. If by some miracle, she *wasn't* dead, and they found her…

I tried to keep calm. That'd be a good thing. I hated killing. And for our part, if it turned out the woman was alive, we'd handle it.

Most likely by leaving as fast as we could.

The mess hall would have seemed like a regular cafeteria, if not for the knowledge that we were trapped in a concrete box deep below the ground. The ceiling, walls, and floor were all cement, with industrial-looking air vents overhead. Round tables were scattered through the space, with plastic chairs of bright yellow, red, or blue beside them. A cafeteria pass-through window took up part of the far wall, with a metal accordion curtain pulled closed over it. Fluorescent lights burned overhead in long panels, and even without my old greliaran abilities, I could hear them buzzing.

Ari barely looked up when I sat down across from her.

"Are you doing okay?" I asked quietly.

She hesitated, her gaze twitching to Harvey. We were back by the corner, while he and the others had taken places closer to the door. Even over the distance, the guy didn't seem to be trying to listen. Instead, he was flipping intently through a moleskin notebook he'd taken from inside his jacket.

"I guess," she allowed.

I waited.

She winced. "Dad, and how he was supposedly a part of…" Her hand made a tiny gesture to the bunker around us.

"Do you remember anything about that?"

She shook her head. "Jace seemed shocked, though. I'm guessing we didn't know. But then, this 'Uncle Mike' business…"

I nodded when she trailed off.

Ari let out a breath. "That was close back there, when Miguel tried to shake your hand. If they touch you—"

I looked away. "I should leave. Go back upstairs or—"

"It'll hurt."

I could feel her worry, and I tried to ignore it because I couldn't fix a damn thing about it. I couldn't make my skin warm to the touch. There wasn't anything else for me to do but leave, even if the distance hurt.

Except that it wasn't only pain for *me* that would be the problem.

"We shouldn't have come here," she whispered.

"They can fix this."

"Maybe."

I scowled.

"What if I helped you?" she asked quietly.

I looked back at her.

"I know you don't want me to, that you want to figure it out for yourself. But if someone here even *touches* you…"

"I'll stay away from them."

"Noah."

Frustration boiled up inside me. "I could *hurt* you," I whispered. "This thing the judges did to you, it feeds off what I am. If you share your magic with me, if I do the same… Ari, what if this pushes you to change or—"

"It's not the same." She shook her head at my confusion. "Your magic. What they wanted. It doesn't feel the same anymore. I can't explain it; I just know it's different. Anyway, Noah, they'll drop this place on you. They'll bury you alive."

"I'll be *fine*."

"Will I?"

I hesitated. I didn't have an answer. My frustration grew, aimed as much at myself as the situation. I wouldn't have air, I'd be underneath who knew how much rock and while, yeah, that wouldn't bother me, Ari might be a very different story.

She might die.

Her hand found mine, her expression becoming pleading and sympathetic at the same time. I fought the urge to pull away. I hated this. We shouldn't be focusing on me right now, not when she'd had her brain torn apart by these bastards. We needed to get this taken care of. Then we wouldn't *have* to be here anymore.

"Noah," she tried.

And I didn't want to feel this again. Not when I knew it'd only go away. Not when her help meant facing the possibility that I'd never figure out how to make it last. That I could be stuck like this forever, longing to feel alive even more than I did already. That I'd begin using her simply to feel like a person again, as if Ari and her magic were some twisted form of a drug for me.

The Beast side of me wanted it. The greliaran side… it just wanted to run away.

"Let me help." Her fingers tightened on my own. "Please."

I'd stopped breathing a while ago, and I was tense enough that it was difficult to start again. I seriously didn't want to do this.

But the way things were right now endangered her too.

My mouth twisted. "Not here. Just in case."

She nodded.

I rose from the chair. Her hand didn't leave mine. We walked toward the door. There had to be an unoccupied room around here somewhere.

Leaning against the wall, Jace tensed when we came closer. Several feet away, Baylie glanced up from the table, confusion on her face. Harvey's expression was the same, but with a lot more nervousness thrown in.

"Um," he started. "What are you—"

"Back in a second," I said.

We fled the room. The hall felt too narrow. Hurrying down it, I spotted a door marked Maintenance Closet.

I scowled. I could only imagine what people would think if they saw us coming out of there. Being called her boyfriend was bad enough. This…

Ari tugged open the door. "Come on," she whispered, pulling me with her. Her free hand flicked a light switch on the wall.

I followed her and then shut the door behind us. Mops and their buckets were shoved into a corner next to a concrete basin with a spigot on the wall above it. Shelves lined three sides of the space, most of them holding jugs of disturbingly bright-colored chemicals, while the light over us was nothing more than a single bulb.

The space was barely enough for two people. We were so close I could feel her breath—quick and nervous on my chest. Her gray eyes skirted past mine, never meeting my gaze, and her hair smelled like the ocean.

I pushed that thought away fast. We'd been in the water yesterday. Of course it did.

A shy uneasiness filtered out from Ari, and irritation rose in me in response. This was awkward as hell and my thoughts were being ridiculous, all because of this absurd location. The sooner we got this over with, the better.

I took her other hand. Reluctance rose in me and I forced it away. Everything else aside, she was right. She could get hurt if these people found out what I was and brought this place down in response.

Her magic flowed out to me, tentative and cautious. My skin warmed, bringing with it an awareness of the cool bite of the air conditioning. The hairs on my arms rose, my body tingling with the sense of being more alive than I'd felt in ages.

But I could feel this draining her. Quickly, the energy inside me spread into her skin to compensate.

Ari's breath caught. Her eyes began to change. A green shimmer ghosted over her cheeks like emerald blush.

I pulled back.

"No," she gasped, her hold tightening.

She squeezed her eyes shut. The magic grew stronger. Stabilized. Her hands in mine were like a flood of sensation. Soft. Strong. Her racing pulse fluttered beneath my fingertips.

The Beast side of me rose up and it was all I could do to hang onto human form. But suddenly, I understood this. I could feel what she was doing, what was changing in me. I absorbed magic, learned from magic, and this was no different. Difficult as hell, yes. Even *looking* like a human was hard—the Beast was massive in scale and shrinking down to human form made a thimble feel spacious by comparison. And when it came to *this*, human appearance alone was like child's play.

But it was possible. If I concentrated right, I could do it.

Elation filled me. I'd be able to feel alive again. Human. Like I'd never died. I hadn't wanted this to go away and now it didn't have to. She—

The room shifted around me. A hallway, cold and sterile. A window, tiny like a porthole in a door. A bed beyond it. A man with light brown hair lying on a blue sheet. Tubes running from his face, his chest. Machines and bloodied bandages beside him, abandoned. Doctors everywhere. Monitors, all of them flatlining. Horror and grief crushing down so strongly I couldn't breathe.

Ari's eyes went wide. She released my hands with a gasp.

The images vanished.

She stumbled back, her hands catching on the shelves like they were the only things keeping her up. Her gaze fell away to search the ground while her eyes changed back to their normal gray.

I didn't move, uncertain what the hell that'd been. "Ari?"

Horror crossed her face and her mouth opened. For a moment, no sound emerged. "Dad… Oh God." She looked up at me. "That was Dad. When he…" Her horror turned to incredulity. "I remember."

I stared at her.

"Car accident," she breathed. "H-he died in a car accident. They wouldn't let me see him. But I snuck by the doctors and I—"

She made a choked sound. I hesitated, not sure how to help. Not sure if I should touch her.

She looked up. "Do it again."

"What?"

"Noah, please. Do it again."

I didn't move. I'd seen her memories. I didn't want that. Good grief, we had enough problems from knowing each other's emotions all the time.

We needed *some* privacy.

Her expression turned desperate. "Noah, I *remembered* him."

"It could've been anything," I protested, feeling desperate too. I knew she needed help. I knew *exactly* how horrible this was for her, not being able to remember her family, and I wanted to fix it. But this might go both ways, and I didn't want her in my memories. With what the Beast had done in its past, half the time I didn't even want *me* in my memories. And as for my greliaran life…

I shoved the thought down. If there was even a *chance* she'd see my past, I couldn't do it. I didn't want to share that part of my history with anyone. Not *that* intimately.

"That might've been some sort of fluke," I pressed on. "There's nothing to say it'll work again. And too much magic could hurt you."

She shook her head. "It's happened before."

I froze.

Ari winced. "In reverse, I mean. In the water the other day, when I was…" She didn't seem able to say it. "I saw a girl. Redhead. You were holding her when she changed into a dehaian. You were afraid she'd die."

I couldn't move. The warmth drained out of my skin, turning it to ice again. I couldn't even pretend to breathe.

"Noah, please," she started.

I couldn't do this. I yanked open the door and escaped into the hall. I needed space. Distance. For once in the insanity my life had become since meeting Ari, I needed absolutely as much distance as I could get.

I fled toward the stairs.

95

7

ARI

I stared after Noah, dumbstruck. I could feel him racing up the stairway, barely keeping to a human speed. The distance ached, but it wasn't the worst thing.

He'd left. My best chance to get my memories back—maybe my *only* chance, if Miguel's people couldn't help.

And he'd just left.

I trembled. I knew I'd scared him. I hadn't meant to, but dropping a bomb on him would've probably been less startling than what I'd said.

But I couldn't have lied. He would have known. For that matter, a heartbeat after I *didn't* tell him, he would've picked up on the fact I was hiding something anyway. We *couldn't lie*.

Besides, what was I supposed to have done? It wasn't like I'd *tried* to see that.

A sensation like a wall pushed at my mind and I stumbled, pain throbbing through me. He was attempting to keep me out, more so than he had since the first day we were connected.

Fury rose, bringing tears to my eyes. Dammit, this wasn't

my fault! My teeth gritting, I threw my anger back at him as hard as I could.

I felt agony shoot through him. Felt him start to lose his grip on human form.

Gasping, I stopped.

The connection was nearly dead between us. Only a residual vibration of pain remained. I quivered, searching tentatively for a hint that he was okay. Still human, at least in appearance, and not *actually* hurt.

A grim sense of confirmation came back, subdued and terse. Wherever he was above me, he stopped moving, leaving the distance at a dull ache.

And I could handle that. I hadn't meant to hurt him. Not really and not like that. I'd just been so upset…

My stomach turned. It wasn't an excuse.

I left the maintenance closet, my legs unsteady beneath me. With a shaking hand, I pulled the door closed. My gaze slid to the stairwell exit at the end of the corridor. I couldn't go after him. Didn't want to, on some level, because there wasn't anything to say and arguing with him would only make this worse. But at the same time, I didn't want to return to the mess hall either. I remembered my father, yes. At least a little bit. But nothing else had changed.

And I'd had enough of those awkward silences and worried questions to last me a lifetime.

Letting out a sharp breath, I pushed away from the door and walked down the hallway, willing my legs not to crumple. I continued past the turn for the mess hall, glancing to the side to confirm that no one had left the room to see me.

Jace stood beside the door, his arms crossed and his shoulder leaned against the wall. Miguel was there too, saying something to him, and Jace greeted the words with a cautious nod. Neither of them seemed to notice me.

I walked faster, escaping the junction before they spotted my presence. I didn't need questions, no matter how many I had of my own.

Because this wasn't fair.

My father's death flashed through my mind again and my eyes stung with tears. Of all my memories, why had *that* been the only one to return? Why not birthdays or Christmases or *anything* else? Why the day he died? The memory was excruciating. The grief crushed me like I'd been hit with a wrecking ball.

I swiped the tears from my eyes. Things hadn't been fair for a long time. He'd been killed by a drunk driver. He'd been stolen from us in a heartbeat. The doctors had done everything they could to save him, but the damage had been too severe.

And he'd been a part of the resistance.

My footsteps slowed. If the judges had wanted him dead, all they would've needed to do was cry "ocean magic" and it would have been over. If Miguel was to be believed, anyway. There was nothing saying Dad's death was a conspiracy.

Why wasn't I sure I believed that?

I leaned against the wall. I didn't know where I was. Some empty corridor with concrete walls, metal pipes, and closed doors with wheels for handles like on a submarine. But it was isolated and, right now, that was all that mattered.

I sank to the floor, pulling my legs to my chest. Why was I thinking like this? My father couldn't have been *murdered*. No one had said anything about him being murdered, not even Miguel.

Maybe they didn't have proof.

Maybe there *wasn't* any proof, because it'd been a drunk driver and things like that happened. Life wasn't fair.

They've had their eye on you for a long time.

I shivered. That man at the judges' lab had said that to me about the Judiciary. But he could've only meant the past year. That was a long time, after all. He could have meant anything.

Like they'd been watching us since they killed my dad. Or even before.

I locked the thoughts down tightly, my stomach roiling. It didn't matter. I'd get my memories back, Miguel's people would figure out how to undo this strakirin thing, and they'd fix it.

If they were trustworthy, anyway. If they weren't lying about my dad and everything else just to get us to trust them so they could use me too.

I hugged my knees to my chest. I'd seen Jace's face. I couldn't remember anything of him to compare his expression to, but that'd seemed like shock to me. Confirmation too. He'd remembered Miguel. He'd remembered what Harvey described.

So there was that—though really, it didn't mean much. We'd trusted people before and been betrayed by them.

I tilted my head back against the wall, wanting to punch something if only to get the frustration out. We didn't have many options. Forcing a judge to help us had always been a dicey proposition. No matter what threats we used, no matter how we tried to control the situation, in the end I'd still be putting myself at a judge's mercy and letting them use their magic on me again. I'd escaped becoming an enforcer once. I was still me, even if my memories were spotty and I had to fight to keep my body from changing. They hadn't destroyed me.

But if we'd gone after Maia's father, they might've tried.

At the far end of the corridor, a woman in a lab coat strode by, only to freeze in alarm at the sight of me. For a heartbeat, she didn't move, almost as if expecting me to lunge up from the ground and come after her. When I didn't, she hurried on.

I watched her go, a surge of exhaustion rushing over me that had nothing to do with how long it'd been since I slept. I wasn't a monster, goddammit. Or I wouldn't be for long. These people would help me. Working with them was the better plan.

It *had* to be the better plan.

"Oh!"

I glanced over to see Harvey stop at the opposite end of the hall, looking startled.

"There you are." He inched a few steps toward me. "You, um, you left. Are you okay?"

I nodded, attempting to ignore the way he watched me like he was afraid I might bite.

"And the, uh, the boy…?" He glanced around like Noah might pop out of the walls.

I couldn't come up with an answer, so I shrugged.

"Ah. Um. Okay. Well, listen, I, um… I wanted to say I'm

sorry for scaring you with the note. We have to be careful, you know? But I know you have to be too, so thank you for trusting us despite my… my miscalculation on that."

I wasn't sure what to say. He was such a nervous person, it made the air feel charged, but right now he was also radiating so much concern that it was hard not to feel sympathetic toward him. He genuinely seemed to mean what he was saying. Like he thought he'd nearly blown some chance for me to get help, and the thought worried him.

"It's okay," I said.

He nodded, appearing relieved.

An awkward silence stretched for a moment. "You knew my dad?" I asked.

"Since I joined forty years ago. He'd worked with Miguel for a long time before I got here." Harvey paused. "He was an incredible asset to the cause."

I blinked. More than forty years in the resistance; Dad must've joined even before he'd met Mom.

I wondered how long he'd been involved in this.

I wondered how much my uncle, Judge Davenport, had known.

My uncomfortable thoughts tried to surface again. "Miguel recruited him too?" I asked, attempting to push past them.

"Oh, yes. He recruited most of us, actually. He, um, he gave me the chance to join after I retired from the CIA. I was an analyst and, uh, Miguel needed someone to help with strategy and scenario evaluation and, um…"

"You were in the CIA?" I couldn't keep the skepticism from

my voice.

"Retired," Harvey emphasized. "Nerves." He fidgeted, his gaze casting around like he was searching for a way off the topic. "But Miguel started this. Him and his brother Alejandro, back in the eighteen hundreds. Alejandro was in love with a girl whose father… well, he wasn't too right in the head. Some kind of mental disorder. But the man started speaking out about the judges, saying all sorts of irrational things—*truly* irrational things, not real accusations—but everyone understood it was only part of his illness.

"Everyone except the judges. They couldn't abide even the *chance* of someone believing the poor man. Next thing you know, the judges claimed he'd gotten into ocean magic. Poisoned the whole family. They, um, they took the girl, her mother, father and all her siblings and, well…"

I could read between the lines.

"The problem was, Alejandro *knew* he couldn't have gotten into that. The man barely left his home because of his condition. But there was nothing Alejandro could do. The judges wouldn't listen. No one would. Several neighbors who wanted favor with the Judiciary even began to insinuate that maybe Alejandro had been exposed too, since he was so 'irrationally' distrusting of the judges. Enforcers started patrolling the area. They stopped him for questioning more than a few times. Meanwhile, the girl, her father, and several siblings all died from their 'treatments' and the rest were never the same."

"Wow," I managed, feeling sick.

Harvey nodded. "But, furious and grieving as Alejandro

was, he had long since started to suspect that the Judiciary had an ulterior motive in all this, and that they might come after him as well. And they did. They came after Miguel too. 'Cross-contamination,' right? Miguel and Alejandro ran. They didn't have family; their parents had died in a Comanche raid on their settlement in Texas about a decade before. They had almost nothing. But over time, they found others like them and built the resistance." He paused. "Enforcers killed Alejandro about five years ago."

I wasn't sure what to say. "I'm sorry to hear that." I bit my lip. I couldn't figure out how to ask about Dad's death. I knew nothing about my father, except for his name and that horrible moment in the emergency department of some hospital. "And my dad? Car accident?"

He blinked. "You remember that? Our reports said there was an eighty—"

"Did they kill him?"

Harvey faltered.

"Did the judges kill him?"

He shifted his weight. "It's hard to know. We do die of other causes and the probabilities are…"

That wasn't a no.

"Listen," he tried. "Are you, um… are you *sure* you're doing okay? I noticed you didn't want to talk about—"

I tensed.

"That." He twisted the edge of his tweed jacket. "But the judges did it, didn't they? Shannon indicated what their next step might be and…" He seemed to search for the words.

"How much did they do? I mean, we don't have any information on how you escaped the laboratory, but we do know the Beast followed you there. We tracked it to the ocean after it broke out, but we lost it when it went too deep. Were you there as well? Did it take you with it? You obviously didn't become an enforcer, but from the planned physical changes Shannon described—"

"I'm fine."

Harvey paused.

I kept my gaze from going to the hall. I couldn't do anything to make them suspect Noah. Not for a moment. But I wished Harvey would shut up. Anyone might hear him. Anyone might have followed him. "The Beast got free. I escaped in the panic. My family and friends had come looking for me. I found them and we ran."

"But the others don't know what happened before that," he filled in.

I didn't want to respond. I couldn't tell if he believed my story; the nervousness on his face was such a constant, it gave away nothing.

He waited.

"No," I said quietly.

I hesitated, a question pressing at me that I wasn't sure how to ask. Or whether I wanted to. "Did Shannon say why they did this to me? What they're after?"

Harvey tugged at his jacket again. "Not exactly. She was brought in at the last minute. But..."

I waited for the guillotine blade to drop.

"But she did seem to think you're not going to be the only one. That they intend to do this to more than just you."

I stared at him.

"Are you sure you're okay?" Harvey pressed.

I looked away.

"I-I'm sorry." He sounded flustered. "I shouldn't push. Dehaians used to need to be near the water or else they died, and enforcers are… well, you know. And like I said, you're obviously not an *enforcer*, but in case you're hurting or… or having trouble controlling it—"

"I'm fine," I repeated, my voice hard.

I glanced back to see him nodding, his expression desperate in its attempt to be reassuring. "We'll do our best," he promised. "Miguel, Declan, everyone. We'll help you in any way we can, and I'll make sure the others know not to tell your family and friends about the rest of it till you're ready—if you have to at all."

I studied him, wary of the kindness. "Thank you."

He nodded again.

A petite redhead in a lab coat appeared at the end of the hall. "Mister Stolberg?"

Harvey turned.

"They're ready for Miss Moreau, sir."

Harvey retreated down the corridor immediately.

My heart climbed into my throat. Just like that, somebody was going to use magic on me to fix what someone else had done.

Again.

I struggled to make myself stand, make my feet move after him. This wasn't like last time. I was trusting these people to undo what had happened to me, yes. But they weren't the judges. I'd be fine.

My gaze darted toward the ceiling before I could stop it. I yanked my focus back to the hallway and strode faster after Harvey. I didn't need Noah with me for this. His presence wouldn't change anything about their tests.

I'd just sort of figured he would be there.

Roughly, I shoved the thought down and kept moving. Harvey cast nervous glances toward me while we wove through the maze of tunnels. We found the others waiting outside the mess hall.

"Where's Noah?" Baylie asked the moment she saw us.

"He went upstairs," I said, continuing after Harvey down the corridor.

She hurried to follow me. "Is something wrong?"

I shook my head.

"Well, is he coming?"

"Up to him."

She took my arm and I stopped. No one had touched me except Noah in a long while, and it felt alarming.

"What happened?" she asked, releasing me.

"Nothing."

She paused, glancing up as if she could see through the ceiling to the house above us. "I'll be right back."

"No, Baylie, it's okay."

She ignored me, already striding off to find the stairwell.

"Ari?" Jace called.

I stared after her for a moment, and then turned, hurrying after Harvey. So what if she talked to Noah? This wasn't a big deal. Noah, me, our fight. It didn't matter. Miguel's people would fix this. They'd fix all of it. I didn't need Noah to bring my memories back.

And I sure as hell didn't need him to be with me now.

8

NOAH

Baylie was coming upstairs. I tried not to scowl.

"Would you like anything to drink? Tea, perhaps?" Fiona asked from the entryway to the sunroom. "A bit of caffeine might help your head."

"No, I'm fine. Thank you."

I heard her leave. Standing by the tall, arched windows of the sunroom, I didn't take my eyes from the rolling hillsides surrounding the mansion. Nothing on them gave any sign of the bunker below, nor of the magical shield I could still feel surrounding the place. It tingled on my skin worse here than downstairs, but it wasn't anything I couldn't handle.

That blast from Ari, on the other hand…

Fiona had been out of the room, thankfully, and the faux-workmen guarding her had been too. They hadn't seen me nearly lose human form. And when Fiona *had* walked in and found me leaning against the wall, I'd told her it was only a headache and that I'd needed air after being downstairs.

I was just glad she seemed to believe me.

Baylie left the library.

"Oh, hello," I heard Fiona say in the hallway. "Headache as well?"

"Um, no," Baylie said. "I'm up here to find—"

"Your friend. Of course. He's in the sunroom. Back of the house."

"Thanks."

Baylie entered the room. I didn't turn around.

"Noah?" She walked closer. "Miguel's people are ready to examine Ari."

That explained the spike of nervousness.

Baylie came to a stop at my side. From the corner of my eye, I could see her studying me. "You guys have a fight?"

I hesitated. "You pick up on it?"

"No, but it seems pretty obvious from your face. Hers too."

I looked away.

"Noah."

My mouth tightened. I glanced toward the door, but Fiona appeared gone. "She can see my memories."

"*What?*"

"Ari saw me, that day in the water with Chloe when she changed for the first time. After the cabin and all that."

"She—"

"I saw the day her father died."

A breath left Baylie. She dropped her gaze to the floor, flabbergasted, and then a confused expression crossed her face. "Hold on." She looked up again. "I thought she couldn't remember her dad?"

I didn't respond.

"But now she can?" Baylie waited. "That was something to do with you?"

My shoulder rose and fell.

"How?"

God, I didn't want to get into that.

Baylie ran a hand through her hair. "So what are you going to do?"

Frustration boiled up in me. "What *can* I do? Stay away from her? I—" The thought was uncomfortable. "She'll get hurt. But she's been seeing things from my past and I didn't even know it until she told me. I can't have her in my mind like that, Baylie. Seeing everything. My feelings. My experiences. Things I'm not proud of. I don't want—"

I shook my head, not even sure what I was trying to say.

"What if you could control it?" she asked.

"What if we can't? What if we…"

I trailed off, my next words hitting me like a brick. What if we lose ourselves entirely? What if we forget whose memories are whose?

And that was it. The crux of the whole problem. I'd already lost my body, lost my life. I had memories from centuries ago and most of the time I couldn't keep my own identity straight in my head. Hell, most of the time I didn't even know what my own identity *was* anymore.

And now this.

"Noah." Baylie put a hand to my shoulder and then froze. "You're not cold."

I struggled to keep from shifting awkwardly. "Ari. Her magic. She helped me figure it out."

Baylie was silent for a moment. "She's having these people help her, so maybe you won't *have* to let her into your head like that. Maybe they'll fix that, and the dehaian stuff, and everything."

"And if they don't?"

"Then you'll figure that out too. But until that happens, I think she'd still want you to be there."

A weird sensation moved through me, like tension and warmth at the same time. "She say that?"

Baylie hesitated. "No, but you're still her friend. You're the only one who can even come near her. I'm guessing she needs that right now."

Guilt twisted in me at her words.

"Come on," she urged.

I nodded reluctantly. "Yeah, okay."

9

ARI

I trailed Harvey along the hall, trying to believe my life didn't consist of making the same mistakes over and over again.

But then, I knew this wasn't like what I'd agreed to let the judges do. It wasn't remotely the same.

Except for how it *really* was.

I swallowed hard. My heart felt like it was trapped in my throat. But I'd handle this. I'd be fine.

Up ahead, Harvey pushed open a door marked Infirmary and then held it while we all came inside. The small room was mostly dark, though a window on the right-hand wall let in light from a second room, this one filled by a row of medical beds. White lights glowed down on the center bed, while beeping machines stood guard all around. Miguel was by the doorway, speaking with a slender woman wearing a lab coat. Pale-skinned, with delicate features, she wore her brunette hair tied up in a loose bun. She smiled at something he said, affection in her expression.

Miguel turned when we came inside, and from the way his

gaze flicked over us, I could tell he noted Baylie and Noah's absence. "Well," he said. "Please feel free to take seats anywhere." He motioned to a line of plastic chairs opposite the window. "Harvey, Willa's expecting you. She's found information on Shannon."

My heart clenched, but no one said anything else while the little man hurried from the room.

"Okay," Miguel continued. "Ari, if you'll follow me, we can get started."

I hesitated. "What are you going to do?"

"Get that magical blob monster out of your head," Declan replied, coming up behind me. "And stop you from becoming a monster too."

"Declan," Miguel said.

The man glowered briefly and then headed for the other room.

"Sorry," Miguel said to me.

I nodded.

"We're going to get a handle on what they did to you," Miguel continued. "Shannon managed to supply us with a brief description of what they were planning for you before we lost contact with her. So we need to know how far along that transfor—"

"To an enforcer?" I cut in fast, my heart racing. "Is that what you mean?"

Miguel paused. My anxiety hadn't been lost on him. I got the impression that not a lot was.

"Yes," he allowed. "That's it exactly."

Gratitude flooded me. I started breathing again.

"Can you reverse that?" Maia asked, her voice pained.

"Hopefully." Miguel glanced over his shoulder when the woman from the other room walked through the door. "Hopefully we can reverse all of it."

"Our examination should give us a better idea of what was done," the woman said.

"Everyone, this is Veronique, my wife." Miguel nodded toward her. "Though Jace and Ari knew her as Vicki."

Jace gave a cautious nod. "Yeah."

The woman smiled at us, her expression warm but strangely sad. "It's really great to see you both again."

I couldn't bring myself to respond.

Declan leaned around the doorway. "Ready?"

Like everything else the man said, the word sounded like an accusation. Veronique paid no attention to him, but simply continued to me, "It won't be the same as the judges' examinations. Don't worry."

I shivered. She gestured for me to go ahead of her through the door.

My gaze twitched to the hall. I tugged it away again. I didn't need Noah here. This wasn't like the judges.

Hanging onto that thought, I walked into the other room. The air inside was cooler than the waiting area, like the air conditioning was working overtime. I could smell antiseptic and latex, along with the bleached and laundered scent of the sheets.

Veronique motioned to the bed. "Just lie down there,

please."

"So, um, will this tell you where the Beast is?" I asked.

Veronique shook her head. "The connection is cut off, so no, probably not. But we also don't want to get too deep into that today. We're simply going to make preliminary observations and get a feel for all the changes the judges have made so we know how to proceed."

I swallowed, my mouth bone-dry. Suddenly, this sounded a lot like what Ellie had done several days ago.

Right before I'd had a seizure and passed out.

My palms felt clammy. I kept making the same mistakes over and over and…

Noah moved down the stairs, coming my way.

Relief bubbled up like a geyser, overwhelming. I stifled the feeling as quick as I could. Whatever his reasons for coming back, they didn't change anything.

I lowered myself onto the bed. Through the window, I could see Jace by the glass, watching me intently. Maia and Dhanya stood near him, and Maia gave me a hopeful smile when she saw my glance.

My stomach twisted. I hoped this didn't force me to change. I didn't ever want those horrible distortions to my body to come back, and certainly not with Jace, Maia, and Dhanya nearby.

Veronique placed several sensors on my arms. "To make sure your vitals stay steady," she explained.

It was hard to keep breathing.

She smiled and then turned to one of the machines, checking it.

Noah came to the entrance of the observation room, Baylie beside him, and his gaze found me through the doorway. His face was tight and his emotions were too: a hard-to-read muddle overlaid with caution.

Fighting back any shred of reaction, I looked away.

"Okay," Veronique said. "This'll only take a moment."

I nodded. Declan came up to the opposite side of the bed. Uneasiness moved through me. Veronique was one thing. She seemed nice. This guy—

He lifted a hand. Magic rolled over me and my breath caught.

It was like mud. Cold. Clammy. Not like the dead-swamp feeling of the judges, but more like a landslide covering me. Panic began to swell through me, making my heart pound, making me feel like I was suffocating.

Other magic joined it. Veronique was standing on the other side of me, her hand raised like Declan's. Her magic wasn't as bad. Smothering and cold but not anywhere near as thick. Like gelatinous mud, seeping in everywhere. I could feel the magic spreading across me, across my mind, searching through me. I couldn't stop myself from flinching away from it.

It was difficult to breathe. So difficult to breathe. The air was thick and it burned too.

My body began to change.

"Stop!" I gasped.

Veronique's magic vanished instantly. Declan didn't move.

The burning grew worse. My toes curled against my sandals. My legs ached like my bones were pulling through my muscles, trying to join with each other. "No." Agony blurred my vision. "Please—"

"Almost done," Declan murmured, his voice tense. "Just one more…"

Noah shoved away from the door. "Dammit, you heard her. Stop!"

My skin was on fire and the air was too. I was starting to change. Here, right in front of my family. I'd see the horror on their faces and the repulsion in their eyes when I—

Fear vanished.

My gaze snapped up to Declan and my hand did as well, grasping his arm hard. A chill coursed through my body, pleasurable like the brief moment when Noah's hands had been on my bare skin.

Declan screamed. He collapsed. Lines of blackish green flew through the veins of his forearm, racing for his chest, and they didn't look like the enforcers' poison. Not really. They were something else. Something new.

Like me.

Other people yelled. Miguel. Noah. I didn't take my eyes from Declan, studying him while he writhed and thrashed on the floor. The poison had reached his face now, climbing through his veins like black ivy. His body spasmed, his back arching and his arms flailing. Only a few more moments and—

Noah grabbed me. Shook me. Shouted my name.

Reality returned in a rush.

I choked, horror hitting me like a wall. I scrambled from the bed, shoving off Noah's hands. I grasped Declan's arm, focusing with everything I had. Ruanir could draw magic in as well as release it. Maybe I still could too.

Oh God, please let me still be able to.

Declan lurched on the ground. The wretched poison began to pour back into me and the black-green color faded from his veins. A gasp entered his lungs, deeper, stronger than before.

I released his arm and scuttled in a retreat on the cold tile floor till my back hit the bed. I couldn't take my eyes from him. His skin was normal now, albeit pale like his blood had been drained. His eyes were squeezed shut, as if even opening them was too difficult.

"Ari."

Noah appeared next to me and I flinched, my gaze still locked on Declan. Sinking down at my side, Noah wrapped his arm around my shoulders. His hand brushed my hair from my face and then he pulled me closer, holding me to his warm chest.

The shaking started, hard and jarring like my bones wanted to flee my body. I'd almost killed somebody. The magic still thrashed like a snake within me, dark and deadly and seeking a target to strike. Because enforcers didn't spare people. Enforcers didn't stop the pain they caused, not unless the judges ordered them too. Apparently, neither did whatever the hell the judges had made me into. The poison I'd unleashed needed a way out, needed someone to kill.

I wanted to throw up.

Noah's hand found mine. The poison suddenly rushed out of me, as if a force of incredible power was siphoning it away. I gasped, looking to him.

His eyes began to go black. He closed them quickly.

Pain scorched through him, even worse than the day he'd saved Maia from the enforcers. I choked, trying not to cry out at the agony of it.

The burning faded as the magic absorbed into him completely. The tension eased from his body and mine, and when he opened his eyes again, their color was restored to dark emerald green.

"You shouldn't touch her," Veronique cautioned.

I turned. She and Miguel were helping Declan to his feet, barely looking our way, while Declan tried without success to shake off their assistance. Jace and the others were in the room too, near the end of the bed and watching us all.

"I'm not afraid of her," Noah replied.

He drew me close again, his hand running over my hair in a soothing motion. Despite his words, I could feel his fear, but it wasn't aimed at getting away from me. I'd terrified him. I couldn't imagine what that had felt like.

I only knew what it'd been from the inside. Numb, dead, with only the shiver of pleasure from fulfilling my purpose to break the cold. I'd enjoyed what I was doing. I'd wanted it to continue.

Worst of all, I'd wanted to do it again.

∾ **10** ∾

NOAH

They got Declan onto one of the beds, and a sharp order from Miguel kept him lying there. Veronique set to checking his heart rate and blood pressure while Miguel used a phone to call Fiona to see if there'd been any sign of the Beast nearby.

I ignored them, not moving away from Ari.

Her family was watching her. No one had said a word. There wasn't any point. Even across the room, they'd seen what happened.

How much like an enforcer she'd become.

The magic twisted through me, weird and strange, but the last vestiges of it were fading into nothing. I wanted to take the rest of it from her, hunt down any trace of it inside her and destroy it once and for all. The way she'd gone cold when it took her over had been just like when the judges had tortured her with their treatments, only with this sick, obedient desire inside her to allow it this time.

It'd been horrifying, like watching this dead-eyed monster take her place inside her mind. I never wanted to feel that from her again.

"Ari?" Veronique tried, walking away from the other bed. Declan was lying on it, muttering curses with one hand pressed to his forehead like he had the headache from hell.

He should've been grateful. He could've been dead.

"Ari," Veronique repeated, "are you okay?"

"Who gives a crap if *she's* okay?" Declan spat.

"Declan, shut up," Veronique snapped without turning around. She let out a breath, clearly working to calm down. "You really shouldn't be so close," she insisted to me. "Ari, I'm sorry, but people shouldn't touch you. If any trace of that leaks out—"

"I'm not leaving her," I said.

The woman's lips thinned.

Miguel hung up the phone. "Fiona says we're clear. No change in the defenses and no sign of the Beast. Wherever the thing is, it doesn't appear to have picked up on that."

Veronique nodded. "Can you get up?" she asked Ari.

Straightening a bit, Ari nodded. We climbed to our feet and I kept my arm around her. She was still shaking. It didn't seem like she could stop.

"You should probably rest," Veronique prompted. "You could lie down here on the bed?"

Ari shook her head, her eyes twitching toward Declan. "I-I'm fine."

Miguel seemed to read her expression. "How about we find you all someplace to stay? We have guest quarters in the east wing of the bunker. They're a bit on the cozy side, but you still might be more comfortable there."

Veronique started to protest, but stopped at Miguel's glance.

Ari nodded tightly.

Jace and the others retreated fast when we started toward the door. A pained feeling radiated from Ari like ripples in agitated water at the sight.

I held her closer.

A few corridors down from the mess hall, Miguel opened another door. Inside, a small and narrow room waited, barely large enough for the three levels of bunk beds on either wall.

"It's not much," Miguel said, "but hopefully we'll get your situation taken care of soon, so you can head up to Fiona's place and not need to stay down here." He gave us a reassuring smile. "I'll check back in a bit, alright?"

Baylie nodded. He left.

No one moved to enter the room.

"Are you okay?" Maia asked Ari faintly.

Ari nodded.

"What was that?" Jace pressed.

"What it looked like," Dhanya said. Jace turned to her. She met his gaze flatly before looking back at Ari, worry tingeing her dark eyes. "You have their powers too."

Ari didn't respond.

"Well, what about the things they were doing?" Jace tried. "Did it help your memory?"

She was silent, her attention still on the floor, though it didn't feel like she was seeing it.

"Ari?" he pressed.

"Give her a minute," I urged. "That wasn't—"

"Why don't you give us *all* one?" Jace retorted. "Clear out and let me speak with my sister alone for one goddamn—"

"No," Ari interrupted.

Jace looked to her, his furious expression faltering into something I couldn't read.

She avoided his eyes. "No, it didn't help." She hesitated. "Noah, can we talk?"

"Ari!" Jace protested.

She headed for the room. He started after her. I stepped in his way and he slammed to a stop before he could run into me. I couldn't figure out what his deal was. He'd barely even looked at his sister these past few days, and he seemed ready to attack anyone and anything that came across his path. He didn't seem angry at Ari, exactly. He was just… seething at the universe.

On one level, I couldn't blame him. This was his sister, and she couldn't even remember him. I got that. But on another level, I was losing patience. I'd felt Ari's confusion at the way he avoided looking at her, talking to her. She didn't know what to make of his behavior, and I didn't know the guy well enough to help her out. And if I asked, the odds were slim he'd tell me the problem, anyway. But he was upsetting her.

Ari sure as hell didn't need that right now.

"A minute," I reiterated, my voice carefully controlled. "She'll talk when she's ready."

Jace turned a furious glare on me. The part of me that was the Beast growled, deep inside, and the greliaran wasn't far behind.

"We'll be out soon," Ari said without looking at anyone.

Jace turned away, fuming. I glanced at Baylie, and then followed Ari, shutting the door behind us.

She stood with her back to me beneath the bright fluorescent lights. I could see her trembling.

"You felt that?" There was only a hint of question in her soft voice. She knew the answer already.

"Yeah."

A shaky breath left her. She turned to me. "I don't want to become this, Noah. Did you see their faces? How scared they were? What if next time I—"

I didn't know what else to do. I pulled her into my arms again. She hugged me, her grip tight on my back while terror pounded through her. I ran my hand over her hair, trying to focus on giving her as much reassurance as I could.

Her breathing became steadier. She didn't leave my arms.

"You figured it out," she murmured.

It took me a moment to realize what she meant. My skin. The warmth. I nodded.

She echoed the motion.

"Let me help you," I said quietly. "Let me see if I can fix this. Find whatever they did inside of you and just… make it stop."

She pulled back, looking up at me. "But what if I see…" She shrugged illustratively.

A sensation moved through me like my gut twisting. I struggled to ignore it. I hated the idea of this, of sharing my past with anyone.

But I'd felt her die inside my mind. I'd felt her turn to

nothing and keep on living.

"Then you see that." I forced out the words. "Me. Whatever."

A breath left her and her gaze dropped from mine, skipping over the floor till it found the only seats in the room. With a shaking hand, she took the edge of the bed and lowered herself onto it.

I reached over, turning the lock above the door handle. They'd hear it, if they were still out there. They'd wonder and—especially in Jace's case—probably get more upset. But Ari might change again, even a little bit. I didn't want anyone walking in if that happened.

I sank down next to her, the springs squeaking faintly beneath the thin mattress. Awkwardness settled between us like an unwelcome spectator to nothing.

"So, um…" Ari started.

"We'll try focusing on you, eh?" I suggested uncomfortably.

She nodded. She reached for my hands and then paused. "I'm sorry I hurt you. Earlier, I mean. After…"

I gave a small shrug. "I'm sorry I freaked out… again."

Her lip twitched, sympathy in the humor. "I just keep throwing you for loops, huh? Every time you turn around…"

I hesitated when she trailed off, her discomfort returning. I could feel the chill in the air, feel the way it made me want to shiver. A quiver like a heartbeat moved in my chest, nothing more than a ghost of what it had once been, but real, nevertheless.

My hands took hers. "It's worth it," I said quietly.

The energy inside me spread to her. Ari's magic flowed back

into me almost instantaneously.

I closed my eyes, concentrating. Beast or greliaran, taking in the magic of others was what I'd been created to do. And I knew what that enforcer poison felt like, and even whatever it was I'd taken in from her. If I could find that, draw it out somehow…

An image flashed past. A red tent. Jace starting a fire. An older man with light brown hair and gray eyes—the dead man, alive now and laughing—pointing out a bird swooping over the desert terrain.

I gritted my teeth, pushing past the memories. Her magic poured into me stronger. I struggled to compensate and not draw in too much. I had to hold the balance between us. I could drain all the energy from things if I wasn't careful. I could—

Dark walls of a café. Maia across the wooden table, fidgeting with her latte and not taking a sip of it. Dhanya coming in the door. Maia smiling, anxiously introducing her.

Jace, younger. So much younger. Offering the teddy bear in his hands.

A city street. Jace, only days ago. Falling, a dart in his neck. Terror. Panic. A biting sensation. Darkness swelling up, taking the street away.

Ari flinched back.

"Don't," I gasped.

Her hands were shaking in mine, but she tightened her grip. I kept my eyes closed. It was there, the sickly black-green tinge of what the judges had done. It twisted through her, tangled around her like a vine, its tendrils sunk into her magic and her core, attempting to overwhelm her with itself.

Ari's breaths were ragged and scared.

I tried to draw the poison in.

Chloe screaming. Cold agony ripping into me, cutting through my body like a thousand knives. Darkness everywhere, all of it alive. Willful destruction that turned to curiosity, keeping me hovering on the edge of death.

Ari made a frightened noise. I held on tight, fighting to focus despite the burning pain of the poison twisting through me. But it was coming out. The stain was growing fainter. It was working.

But not well enough.

The balance between us tipped too far. Her magic cascaded at me, unstable, unstoppable, and totally out of control. Horror overwhelmed me. The poison had gotten into Ari too deeply. Changed Ari to be too much like itself. I couldn't find her anymore, not in the mess of this magic, and if I didn't stop—

I cried out, my hands breaking away from her own.

Ari collapsed onto the bed. Green scaling covered her cheeks, her temples. Her body was likewise transformed, deep emerald with gold, though her clothes hadn't disintegrated and her legs hadn't yet become a tail. Her chest rose and fell in rapid, hitched gasps like she couldn't find air. She stared blankly at the room in front of her with inhuman, snakelike eyes.

I scrambled toward her, terrified. "Ari? Ari, talk to me. Are you okay?"

Her chest spasmed. She was shaking. Cold. Her eyes grew wide, her body locking up as if in a seizure.

I knew this. Remembered thousands of times I'd done this as the Beast. I'd taken too much. She wouldn't survive.

"No, no, no," I begged. "Ari, please. Breathe. Come on."

My hand pressed to the side of her neck, feeling for a pulse. It was weak. Fluttering. Fading.

Desperation surged through me. My magic would feed what they'd done to her. Worse, the poison wasn't absorbed yet. It twisted inside me, horrible and strong and anything I did might return it to her. Might kill her.

I'd *already* killed her if I didn't do something now.

I sent my magic pouring into her.

Ari lurched on the bed. Her eyes widened again. A harsh breath entered her lungs, then another. I tensed, concentrating hard on holding the poison back.

Her fearful gaze moved to me. The draw on my magic shifted, coming from her now and frantic in its strength. I fought with everything I had to keep the balance, to give her whatever she needed and yet keep the poison from slipping out of my grasp.

But I was losing. Her pull on my magic was too strong, too desperate. Fragments of the toxin darted from my grip, racing along the connection between us. I couldn't—

Air rushed from her and the pull on my magic vanished. The tension fled her body and she sagged back onto the mattress, her eyes closing.

"Ari?"

Her green scales faded into human skin. "Did you get it?" she whispered.

Guilt stabbed at me. I could still pick up on the poison twisting within me, painful and strange but less than before. Some of it was back inside her, winding through her like a snake, like nothing we'd done had made the least difference at all.

"Noah?"

"I'm sorry. I took in a lot of it, but some… it was too deep. Too much a part of you. And when I tried…"

I couldn't say it. She'd nearly died. She *would* have died.

Ari opened her eyes. "What?"

I didn't want to speak the words. "I almost *killed* you. You were dying and to stop it, I… Ari, I shared more of my magic with you than I ever have. But the poison wasn't absorbed yet. Some of it went too. And whatever's in me fuels what they did to you, so I probably made this worse and I—"

She shook her head. "Better."

I stopped.

"It's better. Not gone, but…" Her gaze moved around, unfocused as if she was searching inside herself. "I remember. Jace, Maia…" A ragged gasp escaped her. Tears gathered in her eyes. "I remember. Jace gave me a Lego set for my sixth birthday. Maia and I used to lie out in the backyard and name the stars over my dad's house in Arizona. Dhanya's favorite color is green and when we met, she told me she once was grounded for trying to paint her parents' house that color." A smile of wonder crossed Ari's face. "I *remember* them. The judges tried to steal that from me, but I remember. And this… what we did… even if the poison's back, I still feel stronger. Different.

Better."

She looked up at me again. "Your magic doesn't hurt me. It doesn't make this worse. I know they probably meant it to, but… Noah, they wanted you dead. They wanted to take your magic like some kind of fuel, *murder* you, and then control everything that magic does to me. You heard them at the lab; that's been their plan since the beginning. They never intended you to survive long enough to do anything about this. And instead…" A breathless chuckle escaped her. "Instead, you're *not* dead and you're changing this somehow. I can feel that. I *know* that. You're changing this."

I stared down at her, desperately wanting to believe that. I didn't want to hurt her. Nothing in me *ever* wanted to hurt her. This ruanir girl whose people I'd been designed to destroy and instead I wanted to—

Sharply, I turned away, shoving down the thoughts. I could tell where they'd intended to go, and that wasn't going to happen.

That couldn't ever happen.

"Noah?"

I didn't respond, but I also couldn't bring myself to look at her. I'd been an idiot, locking myself in here with a beautiful girl on the bed next to me. *Lying* there, even. And now we had the shock of the last few minutes pounding through us, and the whole thing was screwing with my head. I needed to get a grip.

I needed to get out of here.

"What is it?" Ari pressed.

I stayed silent. Words wouldn't do any good. They wouldn't

fix this, because I should go. Stand up. Put distance between us.

I couldn't move.

Fury rushed through me. I *had* to move. Had to go, because I could see her from the corner of my eye, her golden-brown hair tousled and her raincloud-gray eyes watching me, and I didn't want the emotions that were rising in response. They were difficult. They were all *so* difficult. I couldn't think like that anymore. I *wouldn't*. Last time I'd let myself feel like that, it had cost me my *life* and I refused to ever—

Her hand took mine. The simple action drew my gaze to her like a tether. A strange, questioning feeling came from her, fluttering and tremulous.

I ordered myself to pull away, but my body wasn't listening. I didn't want this, though. I'd died last time and I never—

Her other hand rose. The questioning feeling grew stronger. Her fingertips rested on my cheek, drawing me toward her.

I shivered. I shouldn't be moving closer right now. I needed to stop. I shouldn't…

My lips brushed hers, gentle, soft. Ari's breath caught, longing rising up in her and the awareness of it flooded me. And I couldn't help myself. My fingers slid through her hair, bringing her to me, and I kissed her again, harder and more desperately, drowning in her and not caring to save myself.

Ari's hand took my side, her desire pulling at me, urging me on. I shifted around quickly, joining her on the bed. The scent of her filled my head. Her breasts pressed to my chest while her legs tangled with my own, pulling every inch of her body to mine. My tongue slipped between her lips, exploring her, hungry for her, and her taste was like nothing I'd ever imagined.

Her fingers clutched my side, tugging me to her harder. Her pleasure at my touch felt like a drug burning through me and I desperately craved more.

I took her in my arms, rolling her, and then she was beneath me. My lips left hers, tracing a line down the soft, delicate skin of her throat. She gasped at the sensation, her head tilting back, and she whispered a plea for me to continue.

God, yes.

My hand slipped to her side, teasing at the edge of her shirt. I wanted to touch her. Feel more of her against me. She breathed an encouragement, nodding, making her assent clear. My fingers slid beneath her shirt, caressing her, moving up the smooth, silken skin of her side. I could feel the way her body reacted, the way her pulse quickened and her world drew down to the sensation of my body against hers, my fingertips brushing her skin. Her grip on me tightened, her back arching for me while a soft moan escaped her. My lips found hers again, capturing the sound.

A knock came on the door.

I broke away from her, my mind reeling. Words failed me in my desperate attempt to even remember my own name.

"What?" Ari called, breathless.

"Ari, come on, we need to talk," Jace said, his voice muffled by the thick metal door. "Let us in already."

She swallowed hard, still trying to catch her breath. "Uh…" Her gaze darted from the door to me.

I dropped my forehead to her shoulder. I didn't want this to end. I didn't know how far she wanted to take anything, but right now, her disappointment and mine were making it hard to think.

"Ari?" Jace called.

"Just a minute," Ari tried.

He didn't respond.

I lifted my head. Her eyes met mine, and I couldn't think what to say. I could feel her heartbeat beneath me, gradually slowing, and I could only stare at her in wonder at what had just happened. How fast and how much everything had changed.

And how I had no idea what to do with myself now.

"Whoa," she breathed.

My lip twitched. Hers did as well. She lifted her hand, her fingers coming to rest on the side of my face.

And then sorrow flickered inside her, tingeing her expression.

"What?" I asked, suddenly afraid she was regretting what'd happened between us.

"You… you *died*," Ari whispered. "You told me you became the Beast because you didn't want to, but… you did. You died to save that girl."

I couldn't hold her gaze. I didn't know what to tell her. "Not intentionally."

"But you *would* have. You loved her, even if—"

I rolled off of her, the warm awe of the moment withering. "Can we not talk about this?"

"Noah—"

"Please? I didn't *die*. I mean, I kind of did, but—"

"The Beast *killed* you. Your body, it couldn't have…" A breath left her, the sorrow inside her like a raw ache. "But then the Beast changed its mind."

I closed my eyes. This was what I'd wanted to avoid. This among *so* many other things. I didn't want her to have seen that. Felt that. I—

"It was *curious* about you," Ari said. "Why?"

My jaw worked around. She wasn't going to let up. Or else I'd feel her silent frustration for however long it took me to finally break down and answer her question. "Greliarans and the Beast aren't all that different. We were created to be weapons, to be driven by a need to kill. But the greliaran part of me fought what it was. It—*I*—wanted a normal life. And the Beast liked the idea of having a choice. It never really was fully alive, but it thought maybe together we could be."

"And the greliaran part of you didn't want to die."

I nodded.

She hesitated. "Who was the girl?"

God, I wished we could stop talking about this. "Chloe."

"That dehaian king's girlfriend."

"Now."

Understanding made her go still. A scowl twisted my face.

"It hurt," I admitted. "It hurt like hell. But I can't spend the rest of *however* long I have for a life regretting that. I had to let it go."

From the corner of my eye, I saw her giving me a curious look. I turned away. "Do you believe me?"

Ari hesitated. "Yeah."

She wasn't lying. She just seemed sad. "So is that all why you didn't come back, though?"

I moved to get up. This was absurd. I didn't want to talk about my non-ex-girlfriend after finally letting myself get close to—

Ari's hand caught my arm. "Noah, I'm sorry. I meant, is *dying* and all that why you didn't come back?"

I turned toward her. She pushed away from the bed, propping herself on an elbow and not taking her eyes from me.

I didn't know how to respond. Yes? That having your family know you'd been *dead* sort of made things awkward? That being a centuries-old storm creature was a little hard to explain?

She was still waiting for my answer.

"Yeah."

"But your family—"

"I'm not the same person," I cut in with frustration. "I have this other side of me now, or a new side of the other side… I don't know. Beast or greliaran, I'm not what I was, and to go back like life can just carry on…" I shook my head angrily. "I'm either dead, or a ghost, or… or *something*. But I can't pretend things are the way they used to be."

Ari paused, the strangest feeling coming from her, like sympathy but also wryness. "Why not?"

At my incredulous silence, she sat up farther. "We live for centuries," she said. "We have magic. We're not human." A smile pulled at her lip. "And we go to school. College too, if we want. We get jobs. Have friends. Nothing stops us from joining in on human life except us. Except what we choose to do or not do."

Her hand came to rest on my chest. Beneath her palm, the barest flutter continued like a memory of a heartbeat. "You're not dead, Noah. You've never felt dead to me."

I stared at her, dumbstruck. I couldn't believe that was really possible.

But I'd know if she lied.

The corner of her mouth rose in a smile. She shifted closer, a questioning, sympathetic feeling coming from her.

Her lips touched mine.

The kiss wasn't the same as before. Gentler by far, but with a different, deeper kind of desire. Hungrier, even, yet not in the same way. I wanted to thank her. Show her how much it meant to me, what she'd said. How she made me feel. But there weren't words for it. Words couldn't even come close.

My lips never leaving hers, I took her side, guiding her toward the bed even as her hand found me, pulling on me to do the same.

A pounding came on the door again.

"Ari, dammit," Jace called. "Come on."

A groan of frustration escaped me. "What the hell *is* he?" I growled. "*Psychic?*"

Ari gave a breathless scoff. I drew back, meeting her eyes.

I couldn't sustain my annoyance. The edge of my lip rose while my hand lifted to her cheek. Her skin was so incredibly soft beneath my fingertips.

She gave me a tentative smile. "You really okay with this?" she asked. "Us?"

Longing and desire rose up in me and it was everything I could do not to kiss her again. Her breath caught and her eyes widened at the feeling. I couldn't find a way to communicate how deeply okay I was. I'd fought this. I'd shoved it down and crushed it and pretended it wasn't happening, but that hadn't changed what I'd been feeling for her.

Hadn't stopped how much I was drawn to her.

I managed a nod.

Blinking fast, she smiled again. Letting out a quick breath, she moved to stand.

I rose to my feet as well. She raked her fingers through her hair, attempting to straighten it, and I turned away, unable to watch her without wanting to take her in my arms again.

She seemed to feel it anyway, and a weird, not-remotely-bad tension shivered through her. "Good?" she asked, her voice tight.

I glanced back and nodded. Echoing the motion, she looked to the door.

"What, um… what do you want to tell them?" she continued.

"About us?"

She nodded.

I hesitated. I wasn't sure I was ready to explain this. I wasn't sure how her family or Baylie would react.

"Complicated enough already?" she offered anxiously.

"Oh yeah."

She nodded again, relieved. I was too. "Complicated enough" didn't *begin* to cover it.

Ari started for the door. I followed, bracing myself to pretend like an incredible shift in my life hadn't just happened.

11

LOGAN

Satellites were probably the only things that knew this place existed.

I climbed from the car, scanning the rolling, scrub-brush hills around us. A few miles beyond, the enforcers reported that a mansion waited. I couldn't see a trace of it yet. Some kind of defense mechanism surrounded it, though thankfully the enforcers had spotted it before we had come too close. They said it was an archaic form of magic—something from the *very* old days of the ruanir, something that'd been meant to hide us from the Beast.

It shouldn't have been here. No one had made anything like that in centuries as far as *I* knew. Moreover, for a defense like that to still be working didn't make sense. Ari was traveling with the Beast. There was a good chance she was here, which meant that creature was too. So either the Beast had made it past the defense unscathed, managed not to alert anyone to its presence, and now lurked somewhere inside, or else whoever ran this place had let it past their defenses—in which case why have the barrier at all? Or, third possibility, it'd taken off when it picked up on that odd shield-thing, and thus it was out here with us waiting for her return.

Which, of course, was the worst option. Without Ari in my grasp, I had no leverage over that thing.

I studied the blue sky, finding nothing. Distance from Ari caused the Beast pain, though, and we were several miles from the house. Most likely that counted as being too far from her, given how the guy at the motel claimed the monster had been practically stuck to her like glue. So then, the Beast *must* have made it past the barrier, which meant maybe the defense wasn't designed to keep it out at all.

The possibilities made my head hurt, and they weren't the only thing. There was obviously more going on here than the judges had deigned to tell me. I'd known they viewed me as expendable—a babysitter whose only job was to get the enforcers close to Ari—but this… this was something else entirely.

Who the hell *were* these people?

I ran my thumb over the fake class ring on my finger, its red stone warm from the magical energy trapped inside. It seemed likely that the defenses would pick up on us when we passed through them. Whether or not the Beast had gotten around the barrier, logic dictated that I should err on the side of caution. So I would send the enforcers in ahead of me and watch what happened. After all, even if the Judiciary was so shortsighted that it saw me as expendable, those snakes were infinitely more so.

Hans walked up beside me. "Surveillance reports only one

person has emerged from the house this entire time," he said. "Windows are reflectively coated, however, and there appears to have been some kind of thermal obfuscation installed throughout the building to make it difficult to isolate heat signatures. There could be more people inside the house."

"Who went outside? Willa?"

"Older woman. The scouts believe it may have been Fiona Blackwood, Willa's grandmother. She showed no sign of being aware of our presence. She watered the plants on her porch and then returned to the house."

I didn't bother mentioning she could have been pretending. Even the snakes should have been able to figure that out.

"We have located two other potential egress points," Hans continued.

"Where?"

"A dirt track a half mile south of the property, and another to the north. Neither looks well maintained, though that could be intentional."

I didn't respond. Those had to be exits. Only an idiot would do all this and then leave themselves with only one way to escape.

"The enforcers will fan out," Hans said, his voice lowered. "Surround the area, including the possible escape routes. On your order, they will pass the defense shield and commence taking their positions on the property, at which point you and I will accompany another team toward the house."

I hesitated. Going in the front could be risky. Whoever was in there might attack at the sight of us.

Then again, they may not. Maybe they *would* be inclined to pretend nothing was wrong. A setup like this… they wouldn't want to jeopardize it with hasty action. Maybe they'd hope we'd believe no one else was here and go away.

I nodded to Hans. He gave a short jerk of his head and then motioned to the others. In silence, they moved out.

I returned my attention to the terrain. It'd take the enforcers a few minutes to get to their positions along the shield, and then maybe I'd have the chance to see what this defense was made of. How it reacted. And if I was lucky, once we were inside, I might even be able to get my hands on the source of all that energy.

Maybe even use it somehow.

A smile pulling at my lips, I headed for the car.

12

ARI

I wasn't ready for this.

I'd *never* be ready for this.

With what felt like Herculean effort, I made myself start toward the thick, metal door. The world was waiting out there. My family. A chance to fix things. A chance to change what the judges had done. But I could feel Noah behind me. The connection between us was like a live wire, charged by the memory of his death. Of this girl for whom he'd basically died.

Of his hands on my skin.

I drew a breath. I hadn't been sure what I'd wanted between us before. I hadn't known if he had any feelings for me at all. But when he looked at me with that strange tempest of anger and loneliness inside him, when I touched his face and caught that flash of longing, and when he finally leaned down, his lips ever-so-gently kissing mine…

Live wire wasn't the half of it. I felt like my body was *still* tingling from his touch. I'd never had a reaction to someone like that; never even anything close. Among the ruanir, there were a few guys I'd met who qualified as interesting—and a great number who didn't—but I couldn't imagine losing control of myself with any of them the way I had with Noah. Uncertainty had gone out the window. *Everything* had. The heady rush of his desire had flooded me, fueling mine like a fire, and the effect had been intoxicating. I craved the feeling of his hands on my skin. I wanted nothing between us at all. I was lost to the *world,* and if Jace hadn't interrupted us—

From the corner of my eye, I saw Noah shift his shoulders, a tense feeling of arousal coming from him.

A blush scorched my face. This wouldn't work. We had to go out there. We had to talk to people. We couldn't stay in here.

But I wondered what might happen between us if we did.

I bashed the desire for him down as hard as I could, for his sake as well as mine. After all, we *had* to *go.* The whole of my life was settling into my head like I'd woken up from some bizarre dream in Noah's arms—though I couldn't think about *those* right now, good grief…

Point *was,* I knew my memory had returned. I had to tell the others that fact. My brother, who'd carried me from Judge Engle's house, ocean magic be damned. Maia, who'd invited me to be her maid of honor at the party last week. Dhanya, who'd been family in spirit and finally was going to be family in fact, as well. Baylie, who'd—

Oh my God, Baylie.

I looked back to Noah, desire giving way totally to dread.

"What?" he asked, alarmed.

"You don't think Baylie picked up on that, do you? What

we were doing?"

He shook his head. "No, no way. My connection with her isn't the same as it is with you. Not anywhere close to as strong. We don't really feel anything from each other except whether we're hurt or okay."

I bit my lip.

"Promise," Noah insisted.

I nodded. Taking another breath to steady myself, I flipped the lock above the handle and pulled the door open.

And froze.

They were waiting. Recollections slammed into me at the sight of my family, like everything I remembered was trying to crowd in all at once, just to prove it was there. And the past few minutes, the past few *days*, simply crumbled. Tears sprang up out of nowhere to strangle me. My lungs stopped as the work of breathing instantly became too much for me. I didn't know what to say. *Hi, my memory is back?* It felt so…

Easy. Like after everything that had happened, fixing it had been so effortless—except for the part where Noah said I'd almost died, anyway.

"Ari?" Maia tried. "Are you okay?"

"Yeah." My answer was too fast. Choked as well. I swallowed hard, my gaze going to the hall behind her to check that no one else was nearby. "We, um… we needed to, um…"

"We tried to fix this."

I could have kissed Noah all over again.

"Fix… fix what?" Maia asked. "What happened in the infirmary?"

"And?" Jace demanded.

I faltered at his tone, at the look in his gray eyes. He… he seemed like he was *mad* at me.

The realization stole my breath. My mind felt like a jumble of what I could remember, what I could remember *not* remembering, and things I should have known all along. But that didn't change the anger I could read in his expression.

That didn't change what I'd seen these past few days.

My tears turned hot with confused fury and I struggled to hold them at bay. Even with my memories gone, I hadn't been wrong. Jace's behavior had been anything but normal. Barely speaking, barely even looking at me… and now he appeared mad at me. Or maybe he'd been mad all along. But what was I supposed to have done? Stayed out here in the hall a few minutes ago? Showed him how much of a monster I'd become? Not that he hadn't seen enough already, what with how I'd nearly killed Declan in the infirmary. But what would he have thought about the rest?

"And it sort of worked," I retorted.

He flinched at my tone and confusion flashed over his face. Relief too, but it was swallowed almost immediately by hurt, like he didn't understand why I'd snapped at him.

I stared at him, a ragged breath escaping me. What was *that* reaction? I knew what my brother looked like when he was furious, and he damn well seemed it now. He hadn't spoken to me in days, had barely been able to bring himself to look at me, like I'd been erased from his memory too. But now he—

"So, Ari, you're…" Maia started, snapping me from my

thoughts. "You…"

I was losing the ability to keep up with this. In only half a minute, it had become too overwhelming.

Noah's hand touched the small of my back in silent support. It helped.

"I remember you," I said.

A choked sound left Maia, quickly stifled as she pressed her fist to her mouth. She seemed a heartbeat from throwing her arms around me, and Dhanya put a hand to her side to stop her.

"And what we saw in the infirmary?" Dhanya asked warily.

Noah shifted uncomfortably. "Ari says I changed it." He kept his voice low. "We're not sure how. I could take in some of what they did, but I couldn't get all of it. We're not sure what it means."

"You did *what*?" Baylie demanded.

"I'll be fine."

Baylie didn't seem convinced. She glanced toward me as if seeking confirmation.

Swiping my hand over my teary eyes, I avoided her gaze. The fact I'd been making out with her stepbrother only moments ago felt written all over my face in big, blush-colored marker. I just hoped Noah was right about the vagueness of that connection between them.

Miguel came around the corner. "Hey there."

I flinched, startled, and then memory hit me like a wall and stole my breath all over again. Dad's house. "Uncle Mike" talking with my father in the den. "Aunt Vicki" making dinner with Jace and me in the kitchen. They'd come to visit several times a year—more often than my mother. More often than anyone besides Maia and her mom.

And they'd always arrived at night. They never went outside with us. They always left after midnight, sometimes *long* after, and the curtains were closed when they came by. Dad told us they liked privacy—and that we shouldn't talk to other people about them because it would be rude.

But then one day, the visits stopped. Maybe three years before Dad died, they'd simply stopped. I'd been so upset at the time, and when they didn't even bother to come to Dad's funeral, I'd just…

I was shaking. Noah's hand shifted on my back as he moved closer to me. A breath entered my lungs for the first time in an eternity.

"What are you all still doing out here?" Miguel asked. "I thought you were going to get some rest, Ari."

"Feeling better," I managed. I couldn't tell Miguel I remembered them all. I didn't even know what Veronique and Declan had done. Claiming it had triggered my memory returning could blow up in my face.

"Well… good." Miguel saw my tension. I knew he did. "In that case, Veronique is in the mess hall. If you're feeling up to it, we thought it might be a good idea to talk over what to do now."

I couldn't nod. I didn't want more *tests*. I wanted their help, yes, but I didn't want anybody coming near me with magic again. Except for Noah anyway. That was—

My face began to burn and I shoved the thought aside. I was panicking. I needed to stop.

Miguel watched me a moment longer before turning and walking back toward the mess hall. The others eyed me warily while they started after him.

Jace lingered, almost seeming like he wanted to say something to me—which would have made the first time in days, I thought bitterly. But after a moment, he raked a hand over his hair and turned away, following the others down the hall.

The tears threatened to return.

Noah didn't move. "Ari?" he whispered.

I looked up at him, feeling his concern and then seeing it reflected in his eyes. "I'm fine."

He hesitated, but didn't comment on the lie. "What about Miguel? Do you remember him?"

"Yeah."

"Is he dangerous?"

"I don't know. I don't think so."

Noah nodded, but caution still radiated from him.

I glanced toward the direction Miguel had gone. There weren't many other options. I made myself follow.

Noah stayed close.

Veronique was sitting at a table in the mess hall when we arrived, a glass of water in front of her and Willa seated nearby. Declan was nowhere to be seen, and for that I was grateful. Nearly killing him was one memory I didn't want. But her…

Laughing over chocolate chip cookies. Baking a cake for my birthday.

I hurried to another table.

"Miguel said you wanted to talk about what to do now?" Noah asked Veronique as he sank down into a chair next to me.

His knee brushed mine under the table. Electricity shot through me at the unexpected contact and I froze.

A jangled sense of apology and desire came from him. Not taking his eyes from the others, he carefully moved his leg aside.

I remembered how to breathe.

"Yes," Veronique said. She took a sip of water, something in the motion like she was attempting to steady herself. "Ari… I'm sorry. We can't try again. With what happened, and how your system doesn't seem to react well to our kind of magic…" She shook her head as if recognizing the understatement. "There's nothing we can do."

My mouth moved. That was it? We'd come all this way and that… that was just *it*? "S-so, what can you… I mean…?"

"We still want to help," Veronique assured me. "We do. But what the judges did… it's deep. It's nothing our magic can affect. And it, um…"

"What?"

Veronique reached for her glass of water again as if trying to buy herself more time. I gripped the sides of my chair, fighting not to grab it from her. Fighting not to smash the glass to the ground and make her tell me what she obviously didn't want to say.

"We were able to determine a few things," she admitted. "One, in particular, and we think it's part of why they chose you." She let out a breath. "You haven't gone through the adjustment yet, have you?"

I blinked. I felt myself blink and that was it. The rest of me was suddenly far away, hearing her words as if through a tunnel while ice spread through me. Her question wasn't really a question. She sounded like she already knew. Of its own accord, my head moved back and forth while horror rose up like a monster coming to devour me. I'd worried about this. Not wanted to think about this…

It never stopped. What the judges had done to me. How much worse it got. It just never stopped.

"The changes to your system are extensive, Ari," Veronique said, "and the adjustment… well, after that our bodies become more *fixed*, I guess you could say. Less affected by nature and time and all manner of things. But prior to that, our bodies, our genes, all of it is much more in flux. Much more adaptable and changeable. Add to that the fact your family has a history of judges in its line, powerful ones who seemed more talented than many at handling ocean magic and…"

A hoarse sound escaped me, the only sign of the scream trapped in my throat, choked down below a lump made of incredulous horror.

This couldn't be happening.

"This is part of why we think they chose you," Veronique continued, "and you specifically, rather than your brother or your cousin. Pre-adjustment, with a long line of judges on both sides of your family predisposing you toward an ability to handle ocean magic… you were the ideal candidate. Those alterations they planned are so extreme, it's not a stretch to assume most ruanir wouldn't survive them. But we think they meant to use you as a sort of template. A middle ground, if you will, that would allow them to adapt those changes to a ruanir's system. From what they learn from you, they most likely could spread it to others."

"Spread what?" Maia asked nervously. "They've been making enforcers for years, so why would they need to—"

"What about the adjustment?" I cut in before anyone could tell my family the rest of it. "Will I… I mean, did you find out whether I…"

I couldn't finish, everything in me silently begging her to wake me up from this nightmare.

Veronique cast a quick look to Willa and Miguel, as if she wished she wasn't the one speaking. "No," she acknowledged. "From what we can tell, you won't."

My lungs quivered, forgetting how to breathe.

"I'm sorry, Ari," Veronique said. "Those changes… in light of everything else they've done, the adjustment seems to have stalled. I'm so terribly sorry. I—"

"So what can we do?" I interrupted, fighting panic. I couldn't lose my family like this. Grow old while they were still young. Jace wouldn't even look *forty* by the time I died an old woman.

Noah's hand took mine, only concern coming from him now.

It almost made this worse. He was practically immortal.

"There has to be a way to change this," I insisted. "Whatever the hell they did, there has to be a way to reverse it."

Because I *wasn't* going to lose my family. I wasn't going to lose any hope of exploring whatever this was between me and Noah. I wasn't going to let the judges take this away from me too, not after everything else they'd already done.

I clung to the thought like it was the last scrap of wreckage floating on the open sea. We would fix this. The judges would not destroy my life any more than they already had.

Not like *this*.

"We hope there is," Veronique said.

"How?" I demanded.

Miguel drew a breath. "We go after a judge."

Silence greeted the words.

"Miguel," Willa sputtered. "Are you nuts? We haven't been able to get our hands on a judge in—"

"It's the only way."

Willa stared at him, incredulous. "You've seen the reports. The security they have around those bastards now. We—"

"This is Adam's daughter." He met her eyes flatly.

A shiver went through me at the simple words. At the strange sense of history behind them, beyond the visits I could remember.

"We need their magic if we have any hope of changing this," Miguel continued. "But it isn't hard to assume they'll try to do something to Ari if we let them near her again. It's dicey. We'd have to… well—"

"You'll have to hurt them," Maia cut in. "In order to make them help, you'll have to hurt them."

Miguel looked to her. He paused a heartbeat before he replied, "Yes."

She swallowed tightly. "What judge are you going after?"

"At the moment," Miguel allowed, "we're not sure. Willa's not wrong; they have a tremendous amount of security around them now. They seem to be preparing for something. To get close to any of them—"

"Are you going to kill them?" Maia pressed.

"Not if we don't have to."

She was quiet.

"There are three judges that we know about in this region," Miguel continued, "though the Judiciary may have moved more in since—"

"What about my father?" Maia interrupted.

Miguel paused again, watching her as if gauging her reactions. "We can leave him out of this if you'd prefer."

Maia glanced to Dhanya. "He was the one we were heading toward."

"How were you going to get him to help?"

I didn't take my eyes from her, silently begging her not to even look toward Noah.

She didn't. "We weren't sure. But I might be able to help you reach him. Maybe get him somewhere for you to capture him or something."

"You'd be okay with that?" Miguel asked carefully.

"I'd hope you wouldn't hurt him—and definitely that you wouldn't kill him. But Ari is family. Judges aren't. And we are *so* going to undo this. So how can I help?"

Noah shifted a bit on the chair beside me. I could feel the tangled mix of his confusion and gratitude, same as it'd been a few days ago when we'd met with Ellie. He was glad Maia wanted to help, but he still didn't understand why she was willing to risk her father.

But then, he didn't know about what it'd been like for her, growing up with a judge for a parent. Sure, the privilege was there. Maia's family lived in one of the most exclusive, expensive neighborhoods I'd ever seen. As compensation for their parent's sacrifice in taking on the role of a judge and supposedly saving lives from ocean magic, the kids of judges had everything they could ever want.

Except a parent who felt a single emotion over the fact they'd been born. Or who saw them as anything other than just another ruanir. Or who would experience even a trace of grief if their child died. Maia's father had to be reminded of her name whenever he came to visit, simply because he didn't view the information as important to remember.

It wasn't exactly abuse. It wasn't remotely like what *truly* terrible parents could do. But it also didn't mean she had the same feelings toward him as other kids might have toward their mom or dad.

"You can tell us anything you know about where he's staying," Miguel said, "what his usual security arrangements are. Any detail could be useful."

Maia nodded.

Miguel did as well, more cautiously. "Okay." He glanced to Willa. "In that case, I want you to go apprise Fiona of the situation. Let her know I'm having you run intelligence on this. Then talk with Maia, gather any details you can."

Willa looked away. Her jaw worked around for a second. "Fine."

She shoved away from the table. Harvey appeared at the doorway as she started toward it. Willa pushed past him without a word.

"Last we heard," Miguel continued, "Judge Davenport was in—"

"Um, Miguel?" Harvey interrupted.

I glanced back to the little man. He rocked from one foot to the other, his gaze scurrying around the room and never landing on anything for more than a heartbeat.

"What?" Miguel asked.

Harvey fidgeted so hard with the bottom of his jacket, I thought he might rip it. "C-can I speak with you?"

He wasn't looking at us. He appeared terrified.

Something was wrong. Something *had* to be wrong.

Uneasiness came from Noah, as if he was seeing the same thing. "Everything okay?" he asked.

Harvey flinched. "Yeah. Great. Yeah." His face spasmed toward a smile.

And then he bolted from the room.

"Back in a moment," Miguel allowed. He pushed up from the table and followed the little man outside.

Uncomfortable silence settled between us. Seconds ticked by, turning to minutes. Veronique's attention swung continually from us to the door, as if she couldn't decide whether to follow her husband.

Miguel strode back into the room.

A chill ran through me at the stone-like expression on his face. Something was *really* wrong.

"Veronique," he said. "Declan's morphine is low in the infirmary. Would you go check on it?"

His wife went totally still. "Of course," she replied, her voice so polite and controlled, it was frightening.

She rose to her feet. She didn't look at us while she walked from the room.

Miguel didn't move.

"So, uh, was that what Harvey wanted?" Baylie asked.

"Yes."

The word was cold. Neutral. I saw Baylie not-quite-glance toward us in response.

"Is something wrong?" Dhanya tried.

"We're worried about Declan."

Same tone. I felt the hairs on my arms rise. "Miguel." I rose to my feet while Noah did the same. "Did something change with him that—"

The door to the kitchen swung open and slammed into the wall. Six guys in black military gear rushed in, guns in hand and aimed at us all. Footsteps thudded on the floor on the other side of the room. More people poured through the door from the hallway.

Miguel drew his gun and pointed it straight at Noah's head.

"What is this?" Jace demanded.

The last people through the doors shut them and spun the wheels that served as the handles, sealing us inside.

"I think you know," Miguel replied. "Or he does." He thrust

his chin at Noah. "We found our informant, Shannon. She's alive and she gave us a description of the Beast in its human form."

My heart pounding, I hugged my arms to my middle against the sting of spikes that wanted desperately to grow.

"Move," Miguel ordered, jerking his head at us. "All of you, over there away from him."

Jace, Maia and Dhanya got up and retreated toward the corner Miguel dictated. Watching her stepbrother, Baylie did the same.

I felt Noah urging me to go. I swallowed hard. If he needed to do anything to protect us, the others could get hurt. Space was better for all concerned.

Inching backward, I did as he wanted.

"It's you, isn't it?" Miguel continued to Noah. "Ari's 'boyfriend'. Don't try anything. The bunker's being evacuated and this room is wired. If these doors open without my authorization, this whole place will come down."

Noah wasn't breathing. Neither was I. My focus skipped over the gun-wielding people around us, my heart rate climbing with every muzzle I found pointed our way.

"Don't do this, Miguel," Noah cautioned. "It's not what you think."

The man's expression was like ice. "One move and this is over. Consider that your only warning."

Noah was as still as I'd ever seen him. "You'll die too," he said quietly.

"And we'll protect our people in the process," Miguel replied.

My arms tightened against my stomach.

"What do you want?" Noah asked.

"For you to tell me what's going on. You're protecting her." He twitched his head toward me. "You're traveling with ruanir, none of whom seem afraid of you. They know what you are?"

Noah nodded once.

Miguel glanced to us as if seeking corroboration.

"The Beast," Dhanya confirmed, her voice tense. "And he saved Maia's life. Destroyed an enforcer who poisoned her and stopped their magic from killing her."

"He saved me and Ari too," Jace added carefully. "Repeatedly."

Miguel's expression didn't change. The man was a blank page when he wanted to be, and it gave me chills. "And who's she?" He nodded toward Baylie.

"Just a friend of Ari's," Noah replied.

"Yeah," I agreed when Miguel looked to me. "I've known Baylie for years."

Gratitude came from Noah, though he didn't take his eyes from the man.

"Why are you here?" Miguel asked Noah.

"To help Ari."

"A ruanir." His skepticism was obvious.

Noah paused. "A friend."

The man was silent.

"I'm not a threat to you, Miguel," Noah said. "Not if you don't hurt these people. I'm not interested in restarting some old war."

Miguel's dark gaze flicked over us again. I couldn't tell what was going on behind his eyes.

"Lower your weapons," he ordered without looking to the others around the room.

Body language and expressions alike reflected reluctance, but his people did as they were told.

"So," Miguel continued to Noah. "What do you plan to do now that—"

Alarms blared.

I jumped a mile, spikes rushing from my arms, nearly stabbing me. Lights on the wall flared red. I tried frantically to hide my arms while the people with guns aimed their weapons at us all over again.

"What the hell?" Jace yelled at Miguel.

The man yanked a walkie-talkie from his belt. "What's going on?" he snapped into the receiver.

"*Ari?*"

I turned to find Maia gaping at me and the spikes on my forearms.

"Oh my *God…*" Dhanya stared at me too.

I froze, at a loss for what to do.

"Enforcers at Fiona's," Miguel relayed to his people. "Get this door open. We'll take the south exit. And you…"

I ripped my attention from Maia and Dhanya to see the man watching Noah.

"I can help," Noah said. "If they come after us, I can stop them."

Miguel's jaw muscles jumped. "Last resort," he agreed. "They might not know we're here, but if you show up on their sensors… They're looking for you, same as we were."

Noah nodded.

Miguel reached over, tapping a code into a keypad on the wall, and then jerked his chin toward a man beside him. The guy hauled open the door. Miguel's people rushed from the room.

Jace didn't move. His face was a picture of horror. "Ari, what the *hell*…"

"This way," Miguel called to us. "There's an escape route on the far side of the bunker."

Noah came up to me, ignoring the others. "Breathe." His hands clasped my shoulders. "The spikes will go away if you calm down."

I nodded, working to do as he said. Ragged breaths entered my lungs. The spikes began to creep back into my skin.

I could still feel my family staring at me.

"Come on," Noah said.

Holding me close, he followed Miguel out of the room.

~ 13 ~

LOGAN

When we walked into the house, I could already tell they were on alert.

For one thing, the whole place looked *way* too calm.

"May I help you?" asked a regal-looking old woman. Standing in the corridor beside a narrow table, she appeared to have been in the middle of sorting brochures for the bed and breakfast this place claimed to be. Willa waited nearby, leaning against the wall with one of her hands blocked from view by the wooden tabletop. In the sitting room beyond them, several workmen were ostensibly fixing a thermostat while others made a pretense of cleaning up after repairs to a light overhead.

Swiftly, I debated how to handle the situation. Those workmen reeked of armed security, and the way one or the other of their hands managed to continually stay out of view almost proved it. Willa most likely had a weapon behind that table too. Meanwhile, the old woman didn't look the type to be passively led into anything, nor to be unaware of activities occurring under her own roof.

So there wasn't much chance of shocking them. Not with my knowledge of Ari's presence, nor with the consequences that might result from their actions. The enforcers could take them out—those things were inhumanly fast when they wanted to be—but there was still the chance one of these people would get a shot off and possibly hit me. That wasn't a risk worth taking on any day.

An idea occurred to me. I smiled.

"Hello. We had a few questions for you, if you wouldn't mind?"

"Of course," the old woman replied evenly.

"Excellent. Then may I request that anyone you'd care not to have hear sensitive information be asked to leave?"

The old woman paused. "I only hire ruanir."

My smile didn't waver, though of course I already knew nobody in the room was human. "Well, in that case, I am here on behalf of the Judiciary. We are conducting house-to-house visits to all ruanir citizens whom the judges believe may be in danger, especially those outside major metropolitan areas. I realize this may come as something of a shock, but the judges have learned that the Beast of legend has returned."

Silence greeted my words.

"The Beast," Willa stated after a moment.

"Alarming, I know. Worse, the Judiciary has learned it is in the company of a young ruanir woman. Ariabella Moreau. You may have heard of her? The daughter of the late Adam Moreau and his ex-wife Claudia Corvienne? We believe the Beast has manipulated her into believing it presents her no harm, despite our clear evidence to the contrary. But the creature has a new weapon in its arsenal, one that we suspect has made it difficult for Ariabella to see the monster for what it truly is." I took a breath like the words worried me. "The creature can now appear as a human. A muscular, blond-haired young man of about eighteen or so."

Their stillness took on a different quality. They hadn't known that part; I'd bet on it. What's more, I could see traces of alarm in the workmen's expressions. That thing was here somewhere.

"The Judiciary will protect you," I told them, lowering my voice a bit. "No questions asked. And these enforcers will give their lives to guard you, as is their duty. But that creature is just as insane as the day it was created, and now it is infinitely more capable of stealth. It has already committed several atrocities—" I drew another short breath, as if I was attempting to stay professional despite how much the next words upset me. "—including the cold-blooded murder of my own mother." I met their eyes solemnly. "It seeks all of our destruction, and it has manipulated Ariabella in an attempt to secure that outcome. If you have seen them or have any information, the judges will look favorably upon your assistance."

I let the words sink in, phrasing the request precisely the same way I knew the judges spoke. I wanted the people here to see me as an authority, a simultaneously familiar and yet sympathetic one. And as a possible escape from the position in which they now found themselves.

"Thank you for the information," the old woman replied. "We have not seen Miss Moreau, nor any young man matching that description, but we will be certain to keep an eye out for them."

Her tone was so calm, she obviously was sending a message to everyone in the room. It was difficult not to show my contempt. She made it sound like I'd told her that a dog was missing in the area.

So much for giving her a way out of this.

I sighed. "Thank you. The Judiciary appreciates your assistance. May I ask if you'd like an enforcer to stay with you for your protection?"

No one moved, but I could feel the tension in the room ratchet up another notch.

"That will not be necessary," the old woman replied. "As you said, we are far from metropolitan areas. I doubt such a creature would bother to find us out here, and there are other ruanir who certainly could benefit from your assistance."

I nodded like it made sense. "Very well." I gave them all a smile. "Have a good day."

Motioning briefly to Hans, I started to leave. The other enforcers fell in behind me. Sunlight glared when Hans pulled open the door. I held up a hand to shield my eyes while I walked out onto the broad porch.

"Leave Willa and the old woman alive," I told Hans without looking at him.

I continued over to one of the enormous wooden support pillars of the porch. Shouting broke out behind me. Screams. I leaned back against the far side of the large pillar, my gaze roaming the empty fields, while a window shattered and glass exploded across the porch.

Gunshots popped like firecrackers inside the house and a crash followed. Probably one of the bookcases. Maybe a table. It sounded like wood. I watched a bird swoop over the terrain.

The commotion quieted. I waited another moment, just to be certain, and then shrugged away from the pillar and returned to the open front door.

It looked like a tornado had come through the house. The front bay window was shattered. The console table was in pieces. The brochures that had been on top now lay scattered among the debris. I strolled farther inside. The couch was overturned. Two of the workmen lay dead beside it, while a third was sprawled over the end. An enforcer had collapsed not far from them, his chest a bloodied mess from bullets. The remaining three workmen had made it as far as the hallway. A green stain had spread up through their skin to their faces, and only one of them was still gasping and twitching in a desperate effort to stay alive.

I paused, studying him. I'd never seen a person killed by the enforcers' magic before. I wished I could have been in here to watch it, though of course the gunfire meant that would have been insane.

But it was interesting. The way his body curled with the pain. The way he stared at me, begging silently for my help even though I was his enemy, as if death had made him forget all his priorities, reducing him to base stupidity. It was fascinating.

The man stopped moving. I looked up again, spotting Hans in the hallway. The old woman was seated on the ground beside him, one of her wrists twisted in Hans' grip, while another enforcer had Willa pinned to the living room wall. The enforcer's forearm was crushed against the girl's throat. Her hands clutched at his arm while she fought in vain to break free.

"Now, let's try that again, shall we?" I nodded to the dead workmen. "They've seen—sorry, they *saw*—the Beast in its human form. That look in their eyes when I described it was proof enough. That means you've most likely seen it too." I regarded Willa. "Tell me where it is."

Scorn twisted her face. "Go to hell, you pathetic—"

The enforcer pressed his forearm tighter to her throat.

I glanced to her grandmother. I could read that pride in the old woman's eyes. That arrogance, despite the pain she must have been feeling from the enforcer's hold. This was a ruanir who'd probably been around for three hundred years or more, which meant there was no telling what she'd already survived. She wouldn't break. Not easily, and certainly not quickly.

But Willa, on the other hand…

"Tell me where it is," I repeated to Willa, "or watch your grandmother die."

A warm feeling spread through me at the fear that flashed through her eyes. I nodded to Hans.

The old woman gasped. A green stain crept across her skin, the discoloration extending from Hans' grasp on her wrist.

Willa made a choked noise, struggling against the enforcer's grip.

"An employee at a motel saw you leave with Ariabella only hours ago," I said calmly. "Your defenses outside date back to the original war. You were prepared for the Beast's arrival and show no signs of having fought it off, so either it was here and left, or it's still in hiding somewhere nearby." I grinned, my pleasure anything but feigned. "Continue to lie to me, Willa. It makes no difference to me whether your grandmother survives."

I could see the girl shaking, her breathing rapid, and her blazing blue eyes stared at me with such unbridled hatred, it was amazing. The warm feeling inside me grew. It was like a fire, like heat, that homicidal rage in her eyes. I could bask in it all day. And I'd brought it out of her. I'd taken this otherwise cold and superior bitch and reduced her to powerlessness, to helpless fury.

It was beautiful. I so rarely got to experience this feeling that I found myself struggling against the impulse to laugh at the sheer *perfection* of it.

"Wilhelmina."

The grandmother's gasp broke the moment. Willa's bright blue eyes turned to the old woman and her hate dimmed instantly into anguish. The green stain was spreading. Hans' lip was twitching in the closest I'd ever seen him come to a smile.

"Do it," her grandmother ordered.

Willa appeared shocked.

"Please, Wilhelmina. Do as I say."

The girl shook her head. "But you—"

"Willa." Her grandmother's expression softened. "I'm proud of you. No matter what, know that. I always have been. Now, please, do this for me. Save yourself."

The girl stared at her, a look on her face like she was fighting horror and tears at the same time. I glanced between them, weighing whether to push Willa or let matters take their own course. I wanted to see more of that futile rage.

Her grandmother's expression became gently encouraging, even while her body began to quiver with pain.

Willa gave a jerky nod. Her blue gaze slid back to me.

The hatred returned, but it was different. Agonized and icy, like the girl was summoning up her courage.

Curiosity stirred in me. This didn't seem quite right. Not if she was going to capitulate to my request. Something was—

"Burn in hell, you son of a bitch," Willa spat.

The room went white. I felt something grab me, felt something else slam hard into my side, before gravity shifted and a roaring sound drowned reality. Small things struck my face, struck my arms, and then pain like fire poured along my back.

I choked and opened my eyes. Blue glare. White puffs. Black blur that vanished quickly. I blinked and the image resolved itself.

I was outside. I was lying on the grass and my back hurt like hell. Blinking harder, I rolled to the side, trying to get my bearings.

An enforcer lay next to me. His skin was burned. Blackened in places. His chest moved in harsh gasps, but even as I watched, the motion stilled.

I pushed myself upright, hissing between my teeth as pain flared along my back again. Twisting carefully, I tried to look over my shoulder.

The back of my shirt was torn. Bloodied, and the sight of the damage only seemed to make my back hurt worse. Seeking someone to help me, I glanced toward the house.

The house that was currently going up in flames.

I stared. Smoke poured from the broken first floor window and orange flames licked at the casement like greedy hands trying to claw their way up the outside walls. Past the open front door, the hallway was nothing but fire, while on the support beams of the porch, black and scraggly marks like bare branches were burned across the wood.

What had that girl *done*?

I looked around, but the empty fields and summer sky gave me no answer. This had to be related to that shield, though. Whatever the hell Willa had attacked me with, somehow it had to be connected to the same force that made that barrier.

Or else the world contained two unrelated magical impossibilities the likes of which I'd never seen.

I choked down a breath, pushing my rambling thoughts aside. Willa was dead. That much was certain. The crazy bitch had killed herself and her grandmother rather than talk to me. Meanwhile, the Beast was nowhere to be seen. If it'd been in that house—if *Ari* had been in that house—surely it'd be trying to get her out right now.

Which meant it wasn't here.

Which left me with no leads toward finding it.

My fingers curled in the grass, ripping the stalks up from the dirt.

Something moved at the corner of my eye. I looked toward

the house again.

Hans stumbled around the edge of the building. Burn marks scorched his arms and face. His shirt was torn, but he kept moving toward me, straightening while he walked as if pulled up by willpower alone.

"Are you hurt, sir?" he called.

"Yeah."

He came up next to me and bent down, examining my back. "Minor cuts from hitting the ground. No stitches should be necessary."

I resisted the urge to protest there was nothing minor about this. It hurt like hell, which meant the lazy bastard better damn well give me stitches if that's what I needed.

But there'd be time enough to report him to the Judiciary later. "What happened in there?"

The man glanced to the house. "Willa Blackwood, sir. She seems to possess an unusual form of magic. It incinerated several enforcers, and killed the one who evacuated you from the house." He nodded toward the body near me.

"And Willa and her grandmother?"

"Fiona Blackwood is dead. The attack meant for me had the consequence of also killing her. I was, however, able to avoid the blast by—"

"What about Willa?" I interrupted, not giving a damn. He was here. He had a job to do. How he survived was irrelevant.

"She escaped through the back window, sir."

I stared at him. "She's not dead?"

"No, sir."

I looked around, half-expecting that psycho to appear from the grass. "Get me out of here."

Hans paused. "Sir, you should know that within moments of the explosion, the other enforcers reported noises in the vicinity of the exits we identified. We believe the Blackwoods had confidants in the area—ones with whom Willa might try to rendezvous."

I turned away, scanning the fields and sky. And I cared about those noises why? The Beast wasn't here. We'd driven all day, nearly gotten blown up, and that damn superpowered nightmare in a human suit wasn't even—

Here.

Wait.

An urge to scoff hit me. Oh, that bitch. That stupid bitch distracting me from the obvious.

The Beast could look *human*. Of *course* it could still be here. Those dead workmen in the house had seen it. They'd seen Ari too.

"Get the car," I ordered Hans.

"Yes, sir." His footsteps crunched on the gravel as he walked away.

I braced myself on the ground and levered myself upright, hissing through my teeth while I moved. I'd stay out of the way. Wait till the enforcers took care of whomever was hiding out in those fields, because while Willa might be the only one with those freaky powers—her grandmother hadn't blown us up, after all; hadn't even acted like she could—she also might have superpowered friends.

But maybe this time I'd get the chance to see how they did it. Watch it from a distance. Maybe even have the enforcers capture Willa or one of the others. Ruanir powers took some time to recharge, after all. Maybe these did too.

So I would figure out how that worked. This wasn't a setback at all. This was progress. Hell, this could be *Christmas*. The Judiciary didn't have anything like this. No one did. I could still find the Beast, find Ari, and once I determined how this power worked, I could turn that on the Beast as well.

Or anyone. Anyone at all. Even the judges, if they thought they could keep treating me as expendable. I'd always known I was meant for greatness and power. I'd always known I wasn't like others, human or ruanir. Apparently, fate or destiny or whatever agreed.

I chuckled to myself. Oh, this was going to be good.

～ 14 ～

ARI

"South and north routes still clear?" Miguel asked as he jogged up the steps.

He put his hand to his ear, waiting for the response through the small speaker there. His quiet voice sounded strange against the cement walls of the stairwell and his people kept adjusting their weapons like they were still undecided about whether to shoot at us.

"Fine," Miguel replied to whatever he heard on the other end of the line. "Two minutes till we're out. Lock down the bunker behind us. Full alert. If the enforcers locate the entrance, I want the explosives triggered. Nothing left for them to find—and maybe take a few of them with it." He paused. "Fiona and Willa know the drill. They'll get out."

He dropped his hand from the small device and glanced to the space behind me. I didn't follow his gaze. My family was there. The spikes were gone from my arms, but that hadn't stopped the others from staring. No one had pressed the issue yet, and I knew why. They were waiting till we were safe, till we'd cleared this narrow stairwell of the evacuation route and got past whatever lay beyond.

Then the questions would begin.

We reached the top of the steps and, with a nod to his people, Miguel pushed open a door. A cave lay beyond, lit by strip lights overhead. The space was huge, stretching ahead of us in an expanse of concrete and rock walls that looked like it had been designed as a staging ground for a small army. A ramp led up to a garage door at the far end, while several vehicles waited in between: two cars, a heavy-duty truck, and two SUVs. Maia's own SUV was parked beyond them, tucked between the wall and the farthest vehicle.

Harvey stood by the cars, rocking his weight side to side like a metronome.

"Veronique?" Miguel asked him.

"Just called. She and Declan are clear. They'll meet us at the rendezvous point."

Some of the tension seemed to melt from Miguel. "Good. Any word from—"

A dull boom echoed from behind us.

I froze. Dust ghosted down from the ceiling. The lights overhead shuddered and then began to sway gently.

Miguel swore under his breath. "Status?" he demanded of the speaker in his ear.

He waited. For a long moment, I couldn't tell if any response came.

"House is gone," he said succinctly.

Air fled my lungs.

Harvey's hands choked the edge of his jacket. "Enforcers have already spread beyond the mansion, Miguel. The lookouts had to run several minutes ago. No sign of Willa or Fiona."

Miguel scowled. "Okay." He tossed a look to one of his people. "You. Go with Harvey, Maia and Dhanya; take the brown SUV. Jace and Baylie can ride in the blue car and I'll take Ari and her friend in the—"

"Wait," Jace started. "I'm not—"

"There isn't enough room in a single car for all of you," Miguel interrupted, "and by this point, it isn't a stretch to assume the judges will be searching for Maia's SUV."

Noah looked away. I could feel the frustration rolling off him, even if Miguel's words only corroborated his theory from earlier.

Jace's expression wasn't much different. "I'm staying with Ari."

"And I am too," Baylie added, her eyes not quite twitching to her stepbrother.

Miguel let out a breath. "Fine. The four of you ride with me. Harvey and the girls will trail us in Harvey's SUV and the rest of you split off once we reach the main road. Take the northern route toward the rendezvous point at Calumet Bay, got it?"

His people nodded and then raced for the vehicles. At the door of Miguel's black truck, Jace paused, and I could almost read the thoughts racing behind his eyes. I was still contagious to him. Still had ocean magic inside me.

He took the passenger seat beside Miguel without a word. Baylie joined me and Noah in the narrow confines of the back, with me sandwiched in the middle between them.

Doors slammed around us. The engine of Miguel's truck roared to life. From the beat-up brown SUV, Maia looked out the window at us, her face a picture of worry.

My stomach twisted. They'd be fine. We all would. We must be a half mile or more away from the house. Even if the enforcers were searching outside the mansion, there was every possibility they hadn't come this far yet.

Noah reached for the window controls, rolling down the window nearest to him when the engine started. Miguel glanced back. Noah met his eyes without a word.

The man pulled his focus to the rest of us. "Ready?"

I nodded tightly. Miguel turned to the front and typed something on a keypad attached to the dashboard.

Lights turned green on either side of the garage door ahead. Sunlight pierced the dimness of the cave when the door rolled upward. I felt like we were sitting at the starting line of some psychotic race.

A possibly deadly one.

Noah reached over, his hand taking mine. At the small contact, I remembered to breathe, and my fingers squeezed down on his while I glanced to him. His jaw muscles jumping, he kept his eyes on the steadily rising door.

A hillside came into view, sloping up only a few yards from the entrance. Grass and dead roots hung over the entrance like a ragged curtain, obscuring it. I could see immediately how the entire effect would hide the garage exit from sight of the surrounding countryside. An overgrown path ran alongside the door, extending off on either side of us, while the slope of rough grass ahead was like a trench holding us in.

The blue sedan surged up the ramp and out into the sunlight, ripping through the roots and grass over the garage opening. Miguel sent us racing after it. His black truck bounced onto the path, jostling us wildly. Momentum shoved me sideways into Noah when Miguel whipped the vehicle around the turn. The sharp slope of the hillside rushed up beside the window, inches from the glass. Roots snagged at the truck's siding. And then we were flying down the path, leaving the garage behind.

Enforcers appeared on the slopes ahead of us.

All my hope that this would be simple instantly died.

Immediately, one of the enforcers launched themselves into the air. With inhuman reflexes, he landed on the roof of the blue sedan ahead of us and dove for the sunroof.

He didn't make it far. Lurching backward, he recoiled as though he'd been shot. Momentum and gravity took over then, toppling him from the roof. Boneless, he tumbled onto the road.

There wasn't a way to avoid him.

Baylie cried out in horror as our truck struck him, swallowing him beneath the wheels and then bounding over his body. I clenched Noah's hand, nausea racing up my throat.

I didn't have long to feel sick. A second enforcer jumped from the hillside at us, leaping through the air like a wild animal. Miguel swerved, but we didn't stand a chance. The man slammed down onto the roof. The window beside Jace shattered as the enforcer drove a fist through it.

Noah lunged forward. Miguel was faster. One hand still on the wheel, he yanked a gun from the holster at his side. The enforcer reached in with inhuman speed toward Jace.

Miguel put a bullet straight through the man's head.

I gasped, the gunshot ringing in my ears and the image of what'd just happened burned into my mind. The body rolled from the truck and tumbled away.

"You okay?" Miguel yelled to Jace.

My brother nodded, but his motions looked jerky. I opened my mouth to call out to him when a shout went up from the hillside. The other enforcers hadn't even paused. Running along the rise at a speed so much faster than any human could move, they fought to keep pace with us while the nearest one pointed at Miguel's truck

Four more enforcers leapt into the air.

I heard Baylie cry out, and then Noah was gone. In midair, the enforcers stopped as though something had snagged them, and then they were flying backward, screaming while they disappeared over the rise. More charged at us only to be caught before they could leap from the hillside.

Miguel swore. I turned to see an enforcer slip down to the road directly in front of us, not jumping, not making a move to be noticed till the final second. I felt Noah whirl around, felt him surge toward us when he realized their trick, but the enforcer was already coming. Leaping up from the road like gravity meant nothing, the man charged over the hood of the truck, over the roof. With one hand gripping the metal roof like he was glued to it, the enforcer swung himself into the truck bed.

Noah raced down. Glass shattered behind me. I scrambled forward, trying to get beyond the enforcer's reach.

A hand landed on the back of my neck.

Ice flooded me, stealing thought, stealing fear. Time slowed. I could feel my heart, the beats a thousand years apart, and my exhaled breath was the only sound. Glass bits hung in the air. My connection to Noah went flat. Around me, everyone was frozen and so desperately vulnerable, and suddenly, it was all so simple. So incredibly simple.

Cold ecstasy chilled me to my core. I wanted this. I'd been made for this.

But it wasn't like before.

I spun and grabbed the enforcer behind me. A frigid thrill shot through my veins, like ice water from the depths of the world.

The man flew backward. His body slammed into the hillside in a fountain of dirt and rock.

Time and warmth and sound returned. The trench came to an end, ejecting the SUV up a short slope and onto a concrete road. Noah reappeared beside me. I felt his shock.

I couldn't take my eyes from the body crumpled by the roadside.

"Ari?" Noah said.

"What the *hell* was that?" Baylie cried.

Miguel veered the truck around a turn. The body disappeared behind the curve.

A rough breath entered my lungs. "Jace, are you okay?" I

called.

Silence followed. I tugged my attention from the road to find my brother staring at me. Blood splattered his face. He looked white as death.

"Y-yeah," Jace managed. "The guy didn't touch me."

"*Ari*," Noah repeated.

I didn't respond. I wasn't sure what to say. Alarm was inside me somewhere, tangled up in a new, cold certainty that I'd done what was necessary. What was right.

And that what the enforcer had tried… it'd been meant to turn me on the others. I knew it as clearly as if their deaths had happened right before my eyes. I'd felt the enforcer's magic pour into me, slamming down like a weight on a perilously balanced scale and hurtling me toward oblivion.

But something else had gotten in the way. Something had held on, restraining me by its fingernails from the edge of the abyss and letting me keep the barest scrap of my free will. I'd still craved it, still felt that horrible pleasure at killing, and everything in me seemed shaky in a way it hadn't been before. But I'd managed to control my response to what the enforcer had attempted to do.

I trembled, my stomach roiling. My gaze slid toward Noah. He watched me, worried and silently questioning.

"You changed it," I whispered.

Cautious relief threaded through his concern, like it wasn't certain it should be there. Warily, he wrapped his arm around my shoulders, pulling me to him.

I sank into his embrace. From the corner of my eye, I could

see Baylie and Jace watching me.

Miguel steered the truck onto a main road. The empty landscape that hid the bunker fell behind us and there wasn't an enforcer or a judge to be seen.

I turned my face away, closing my eyes and wishing I knew what to do now.

❧ 15 ❧

LOGAN

My car rolled to a stop in front of the group of enforcers and immediately I could tell they'd failed.

For one thing, I didn't see anyone *besides* enforcers anywhere.

Shoving the door open, I climbed out. "What happened?"

"We were correct," Hans said. "Several vehicles attempted to escape via the exits we'd marked and, unfortunately, they were successful. But the enforcers were able to identify some of the individuals in those vehicles—including one who appeared to be Miguel Salazar."

I stared at him, hearing the emphasis in his tone. Okay… and I was supposed to know who that was *how?*

"He is an enemy of the ruanir and wanted by the Judiciary," Hans said, as if reading my silent derision.

"Right." I glanced back toward the cars, not particularly caring. Sure, "enemy of the ruanir" was about on the level of being called a terrorist or the FBI's Most Wanted or whatever, but that wasn't the problem. "And you lost him."

"They had assistance. Ariabella and the Beast were also

present."

"Wait, *what?*"

"They were in the vehicle with Salazar. They escaped with him, sir."

I'd been right. The Beast had been here.

And these enforcers were *still* here. "What did your men do? Run away? How could you let them just—"

"Several of our number died, sir," Hans stated, a note in his voice that I'd swear was reproach. "The enforcers attempted to trigger the last stages of transformation in the subject, but—" The man grimaced. He actually *grimaced*. I couldn't believe this. "It failed. She turned on us instead. We do not know why."

I scoffed. He didn't know why. Like that damn well mattered.

"So now what?" I snapped. "Where'd they go? Did your people manage *anything* in terms of slowing them down or figuring out where they're heading?"

"The Judiciary needs to be informed, sir."

I stared at him. That wasn't an answer.

He didn't have an answer.

"Yeah," I agreed coldly. "And maybe they'll send me some people who can actually do their jobs."

I turned away. I knew he wouldn't do anything to me. He *couldn't*, not when I represented the Judiciary. And they'd be as disgusted with him as I was.

Pulling my phone from my pocket, I walked several steps away from him. A moment passed before Judge Engle answered.

"Report."

"The enforcers you sent with me failed. Ariabella and the

Beast were here, but the enforcers didn't want to risk themselves enough to stop them. Instead, they let the targets escape with the insurrectionists and some guy named Miguel Salazar."

Silence answered me.

"Sir?"

"The enforcers are *certain* it was Salazar?"

Surely, that wasn't the important part of this? "Hans claimed that, yes. But sir, the Beast and Ariabella were—"

"Yes, Mister Marseilles, you made that clear. But if Miguel Salazar is there, then we all have a much larger problem than previously anticipated."

I paused. "Sir?"

"Miguel Salazar is the founder of the subversive forces about whom I warned you. He is a deranged, bloodthirsty insurrectionist who will stop at nothing to overthrow the Judiciary and destroy our entire way of life. He was also believed to have been dead for over a decade. For him to be back now with the power of the Beast at his disposal is a significant development."

I hesitated. Okay, well yeah, that did sound like a problem. This guy was apparently insane, and the enforcers I was babysitting had screwed up, leaving *me* looking responsible for letting him go.

Meanwhile, this nut-job's people were the ones with this new magic.

Shit.

My thoughts raced, attempting to figure out how to turn this to my advantage. There had to be a way. Something that could maintain my position in the Judiciary's good graces, put the blame back on the enforcers where it belonged, and keep me safe at the same time.

I elected to try honesty—to an extent, anyway. I adopted a concerned tone. "There is something else, sir. The people here… they displayed a strange form of magic. A very destructive one."

"Explain."

"They have a barrier around this place, similar to the ocean magic defenses our ancestors used to protect against the Beast. But it doesn't seem to have worked because the creature was here. And one of them, Willa Blackwood… Sir, she blew up her *house* to stop us from questioning her further."

The judge was quiet for a moment. "That is concerning."

I weighed how to respond. "Yes, sir. I'm sure the Judiciary will want to investigate. But sir, these enforcers. Despite failing to capture Ariabella and allowing Miguel Salazar to escape in spite of my best efforts, several of them did die. I would like to request replacements be sent to my location so that I can continue my pursuit."

"Was there any contact with Miss Moreau by the enforcers?"

I fought back a scowl. "Yes. According to Hans, they attempted to trigger the transformation. But they were unsuccessful."

"What happened?"

"They failed, sir." I pitched my voice with plenty of tension and contempt, because like *hell* would I let anyone see this as my fault. "Hans said she turned on them."

The judge was silent.

"Sir, the replacement enforcers—"

"Thank you for the information, Mister Marseilles. I have a new destination for you. Put Hans on the phone. I will give him the directions."

For a brief moment, I didn't move, shocked. Thank you for the information, now put the snake on the phone? That was *it*?

Shit, shit, *shit*.

"Mister Marseilles?"

"Of course, sir," I replied on autopilot. I glanced toward the enforcers.

Hans was watching me.

I walked over to him. "Judge Engle wishes to give you directions for our next destination," I said, meticulously making certain my voice gave no hint of my opinion. Like, say, my outrage at the fact I'd basically been reduced to a *secretary*—one without any damn reinforcements.

Hans took the phone.

I made a point not to move away from him, and I kept my face utterly still. My focus didn't stay on him—that would appear desperate—but instead I turned my attention to the enforcers nearby, like the entire phone conversation was of no consequence to me.

They were carrying the bodies from the side of the road and loading them into the trunks of their various cars. Others were gathering any bloodstained dirt into plastic bags, making sure they left no evidence that corpses had been there only moments before.

"Yes, sir," Hans said. "Understood."

He hung up. I took the phone.

"A secondary plan of the Judiciary's has come to fruition," Hans told me. "They wish us to meet their forces by the coast."

"Forces?"

"For the next stage of the process."

I debated appropriate responses. Okay, more forces would be good. People were blowing up buildings; I wanted all the forces between me and them as I could get. But it didn't take a genius to figure out this "process" thing wasn't going according to plan.

Ari had turned on the damn enforcers, for pity's sake.

Hans was waiting.

"Of course," I said, my voice giving nothing away.

Expressionless, I headed for the car.

This was bullshit.

I let out a breath slowly, working to bring my pounding heart back to a normal speed. I could still use this, though. I was getting more enforcers, at least. The Judiciary obviously thought the ones I had weren't good enough, same as I did. And if Ari and the Beast were heading for the coast, then those magical freaks probably would be too, which meant—after throwing enough enforcers at them to kill this Miguel guy and disable whatever the hell they were able to do—I could get my hands on the source of their power.

All wasn't lost.

I closed the car door. I would use this. I found a way to use everything. I'd never met a problem yet that I couldn't figure out how to solve, no matter how badly it went for the person stupid enough to be in my path. And as far as this process was concerned, well…

My lip twitched. That was good too.

After all, I doubted it was meant to go particularly well for Ari or the Beast.

↬ 16 ↫

NOAH

Ari hadn't spoken for hours. She hadn't even left my side. Wind whipped through the broken windows to tug at her hair, and carefully steady breaths escaped her, doing little to calm the swirl of emotions inside her. I rubbed my hand on her arm, trying my best to comfort her, or maybe just comfort myself. I couldn't make sense of what she was feeling, except to know she was shaken.

She wasn't the only one.

Jace and Baylie hadn't said a word. But for short conversations on his cell phone, Miguel hadn't either. Their uneasiness at what Ari had done was obvious. They'd all been casting quick glances toward Ari and me during the drive toward Calumet Bay, but no one had chosen to press the issue.

I was grateful. I didn't know what to tell them.

My gaze skimmed over the terrain around us, barely seeing it. When Ari had killed that enforcer, she'd moved faster than a dehaian. Faster than me. I'd never seen anything like it in my life—in *either* of my lives. In less than a heartbeat, she'd turned and taken out a full-grown man. And when she was finished, the cold in her had vanished, like she'd managed to control it for the first time. I knew something inside her had shifted when that enforcer had grabbed her. I just didn't have a clue what he'd done.

I stopped myself from twitching with discomfort. Ari was distracted and I didn't want to give her a reason to notice my concern. But it worried me, what the enforcer had tried. He hadn't gone for Baylie, Miguel, or Jace. He'd simply broken the window and grabbed the back of Ari's neck, even though that wouldn't have given him leverage to do anything at all. He must have known there wouldn't be much time, either, with what Miguel's guns or I could do to him. So touching her had been the goal. Just getting a hand on her.

When the judges had her in their lab, they'd kept talking of stages. Given what had happened back there, I had the horrible, sinking feeling that the enforcer touching her had been an attempt to initiate another one.

Except it hadn't gone according to plan.

My hand rubbed Ari's arm harder. She kept changing. Kept *being* changed over and over again by what those bastards had done.

I didn't want to lose her.

From the corner of my eye, I saw Ari glance at me, worry bubbling up in her and directed at me. I locked my attention on the world beyond the window, knowing that talking about it would only make things worse—and bring the others into the conversation.

She shifted a little closer to me and didn't say a word. I buried my relief, keeping my focus on the terrain. It was later than it appeared out there, what with the summer sunset staining the sky, and we were still close to the ocean. I could feel it over the hillsides, beyond all the trees, and I could tell Ari did too. Her head kept turning in that direction before she'd tug her gaze away, and beyond her worry was a tension that seemed to grow stronger with every moment.

It was difficult to hold my frustration down. More than anything, I wanted to take her with me and head as far beneath the water as she could stand. The judges couldn't follow us into the deep ocean, after all, and their enforcers couldn't either. Down there, we might be safe.

But then, Ari wouldn't want to go and it wasn't a long-term solution in any case. It wouldn't fix this and she'd need to change into strakirin form to do it—something that might make her problems worse.

And anyway, it terrified her.

I pulled my focus to the other side of the road, away from the ocean, and did my best to smother my concerns down where hopefully she wouldn't pick up on them. We'd have to come up with something else, some other way to fix this for her.

Miguel's phone buzzed. He thumbed it on and lifted it to his ear. "What?"

I waited, missing my greliaran hearing.

"Take it down." Miguel paused. "You heard me. Yes, it—he—is still with us."

I tensed.

"Yeah, we're a few minutes out." Another pause. "You have her?" A longer pause this time, and when he spoke again, anger threaded through his tone. "Whatever she needs. Just bring her there with you and try to keep her resting for as long as you can. But—" He hesitated. "Don't tell her where you're taking her. Just in case."

He hung up.

Jace looked to him with a cautious expression. "Who?"

"Shannon."

"Is she dangerous?"

Miguel didn't answer for a moment. "Simply playing it safe. It'll be okay."

I looked to the window, not feeling remotely reassured. Whatever else he might be, Miguel clearly wasn't stupid: the enforcers had found the hideout for a reason.

Flicking the turn signal, Miguel guided the truck onto a narrow road leading from the highway. Behind us, Harvey's brown SUV followed.

No one said another word.

Minutes ticked past while the landscape gradually became more overgrown and forested. Miguel steered along a winding path until finally a chain-link gate across the road slowed us. When we pulled close, the gate lurched and then drew aside. I checked around quickly, scanning the woods, and spotted a small camera perched some distance ahead.

Miguel kept driving.

The road twisted onward, rough and potholed, like it hadn't

been used in years. A tunnel of spruce and ferns surrounded us, but as the minutes crept on, space began to open up beyond the trees. Clouds glowing in the dying sunset looked back at us. Glimpses of darkening water beneath them hinted at the ocean.

And then we came around a turn and it was there.

I felt Ari take a rough breath beside me. Up ahead, a large swath of land had once been cleared to make space for a two-story house, though nature had obviously tried to rectify the situation. Weeds and overgrown bushes snarled the landscape around a weathered fence that was missing more boards than it still possessed. The house itself seemed on the verge of collapse, with some of its siding hanging loose and what looked like a hole in its roof. Tatters of sun-bleached, blue tarps still clung valiantly to several window frames, nailed in place an untold amount of time before. A large equipment shed occupied the opposite side of the overgrown lawn; the building appeared to be as dilapidated as the house.

And beyond it all was the ocean.

In spite of myself, my gaze lingered on it. A couple hundred yards probably separated us from the water, maybe more. The ground ended with a cliff where the ocean had steadily chewed away at the coastline. A lighthouse of white stone stood near the edge like a stalwart guard, in better shape than the house, yet still weathered by decades of overlooking the sea.

But the water was there, just there, with all the relative safety it could provide.

I tugged my attention away from it. Beside me, Ari shivered, her eyes locked on the truck's floor.

Miguel guided the truck behind the storage shed and then pulled inside. Shadows surrounded us. Without a word, he turned off the engine and then pushed his door open.

Ari straightened, her eyes not meeting mine or anyone else's. Her hand moved to take my own, though. Holding onto her, I climbed from the truck. Shadows clustered thick in the storage building, although I could still see the cobwebs plastering the ceiling. They hung down in long, dust-fuzzed tendrils.

I paused, catching sight of a glint overhead. A camera, tiny and barely noticeable, fastened its lens on us. Other cameras dotted the upper reaches of the corners, so small that they could almost have been mistaken for bugs.

The brown SUV pulled in beside us. Maia and Dhanya hurried out.

"You guys okay?" Maia asked.

Ari nodded.

"Yeah," Jace answered. "Fine."

He glanced to Miguel.

"This way," the man said.

Still keeping Ari's hand in mine, I followed Miguel from the shed, attempting to ignore the questions I could see passing between the others in silent glances.

We walked toward the house on a narrow track through the brambles. The building was even more rundown up close. Shingles from its roof dotted the overgrown lawn, their reddish color nearly lost beneath a coating of mildew and moss. Small poles were tucked into the grass near them, however, with a rough scrawl of symbols on their sides that looked similar to the markings on the defenses outside Fiona's place.

I buried a scowl.

We started up onto the porch. The wooden siding ahead of us was splintered and cracked, and weathered flakes of white paint still clung to it. Behind their shredded tarps, several of the nearby windows had shattered; only shadows and darkness lay beyond them. The planks of the steps sagged as if threatening to give way. I heard Maia take a short breath when one of them creaked alarmingly beneath her foot. Overhead, the porch roof appeared equally unstable, as if the weight of a sparrow might send it crashing down.

Miguel paused at the door and bent down. Tugging aside a floorboard, he revealed a tiny keypad tucked below it. Swiftly typing in a series of numbers, he waited only long enough for the light on the pad to go green, and then he put the slat back in place.

Without a word, he took the handle and opened the door.

An entirely different house waited inside.

I tried to keep my jaw from dropping. The walls were bone-white and appeared to be formed of concrete rather than drywall. The door was at least three times as thick as it'd appeared from the outside, and reinforced with metal plating. Though they'd seemed broken from the porch, the windows were actually blocked by sheets of metal as well. Heavy-duty hinges ran along one side of the coverings and the opposite side was bolted down with a series of massive locks, as if a steel door had been shut over each window. At the top of the stairway, a large trapdoor was closed over the entire stairwell, blocking the upstairs from access. A rack of rifles and shotguns took up one wall, while the other walls supported flat-panel televisions. Black-and-white images of the yard and shed showed on all of the screens; there were at least a dozen more cameras outside than the ones I'd spotted.

It was difficult not to stare. The place looked ready to withstand the apocalypse, let alone the enforcers who had leapt like wild animals from the hillsides to attack us.

"This way." Miguel headed for the stairs to the second floor. I hesitated, glancing to the others warily before following.

The next level was much like the first, all steel plating and white surfaces. The interior walls toward the front of the house had been gutted, leaving a large open room, while toward the back, they had been left intact. Closed doors blocked access to whatever lay at the rear of the house. Desks occupied the space to my left, while more flat-screen televisions hung over them, though unlike downstairs, these screens displayed news reports. People sat in chairs beneath the monitors, studying the news and the laptops on their desks with equal intensity. In a corner away from them all, Declan sagged in a wooden chair, a glower etched on his narrow face. Veronique stood by the nearest desk, a phone to her ear.

"That's excellent, thank you." She hung up and turned. Relief flashed over her face when she saw Miguel.

Her expression faltered at the sight of me. "Um, so…"

Declan made an angry noise. "You could have *told* us you were bringing that—"

"Enough," Miguel interrupted. "He's here."

"But the energy we wasted—"

"I said *enough*."

The room went quiet. I watched the members of the resistance, ready to lose human form at the first hint of hostility.

They didn't move. Not a single one took their eyes from me.

"This is the Beast," Miguel said. "Apparently, he goes by Noah. And until further notice, we are treating him as a guest, because I *really* don't want to start a fight, understood?"

Silence followed.

"*Understood?*"

Sounds of agreement came from around the room. Declan looked away, scowling.

"Good. Now, has there been any word from Willa or Fiona?"

Veronique hesitated. "No. We've had trouble getting anyone close to the house, though. None of the sensors have tripped for the bunker, but the enforcers are still swarming the area. And as for the house itself…" She shook her head.

I kept myself from shifting with discomfort. That must have been the explosion we'd felt while we were in the tunnels. The house going down. And there was nothing I could have done to save it or whomever was inside either. Not and protect Ari and Baylie at the same time.

The truth of that didn't make me feel any better.

"But…" Veronique's gaze twitched toward me and Ari before returning to her husband. "If I could speak to you on another matter…?"

Miguel paused. "Does it concern them?" He nodded toward

us.

Veronique was silent, but the answer was clear on her face.

"Then you can tell them too," he said.

Her mouth tightened like she wanted to argue, but after a moment, the expression faded. "There was an attack. A ruanir neighborhood in a small town north of Sacramento. It was on the news. The attackers covered it up by burning the neighborhood and making it look like a wildfire, but…" She exhaled sharply. "Miguel, it was the dehaians. Word spread fast through our communities on the internet. The survivors saw people with spikes, moving fast, carrying dehaian weapons and yelling something about 'enemies of Yvaria'."

Miguel looked away, cursing under his breath.

I wasn't far behind. "It's the judges," I said.

Miguel looked toward me.

"They're working with a group of dehaians," I continued. "Their plan is to convince your people that Yvaria is starting a war. But it's a lie. Yvaria wouldn't do this."

"So says you," Declan spat. He looked to Miguel. "Who the hell is Yvaria?"

"It's a country," I cut in before Miguel could speak. "Not a person. And they're peaceful. They're not behind this."

Declan scoffed. "We're supposed to trust that you—"

"Are you sure?" Miguel interrupted.

"Yes. I know them. They don't control me, but I know them. I already confronted their king about the first attack and he swore they weren't responsible for it." I hesitated. "He's *well* aware of what I could do if I found out he lied to me, Miguel."

For a long moment, Miguel watched me. "Okay."

"Miguel," Veronique started.

Declan made an incredulous noise. "You can't seriously—"

"We can believe it's a new offensive by the dehaians or we can believe it's the enemy we already know. Considering what we've seen, it makes sense to proceed as if it's the latter. So until we find out differently, that's what we're going to do. Am I clear?"

Veronique nodded. Declan turned away, muttering angrily.

"You three," Miguel continued, looking to a trio of people by the computers. "Stay online, see what you can learn about this from the civilian ruanir. You two," he nodded to several others, "question our contacts. Find out any information you can. The rest of you, I want the focus to be on Willa and the attack at Fiona's. Track those enforcers and anyone they—"

The door on the far side of the room opened. A choked gasp followed the sound.

I turned to see a petite blond woman, her face white with alarm. Her hand clutched the door handle with a claw-like grip and she seemed to be shaking. In the room behind her, a row of cots was visible beneath steel-covered windows, though only one of the beds looked slept in.

But I recognized the woman. She'd been at the lab. She'd thrown the switch on the device that drained magic from me. She'd reported about Ari being "ready" for the judges' procedures. And she hadn't even batted an eye. She'd just stood there, cold like ice, knowing what they were going to do and how they would—

Ari's hand grabbed mine and her nails dug into my skin. I tore my attention from the woman long enough to see Ari look up at me, her expression tight with anger and yet imploring me to stay calm.

"Shannon?" Veronique hurried toward her. "I told them to ask you to stay in the back till—"

She reached for the woman's arm, but Shannon only yanked it away, never once glancing in Veronique's direction. The woman's cold, rigid calm from the lab was gone. Now, her eyes were wild. She looked like she was staring at a monster. Like she was a rabbit cornered by a predator, frozen with nowhere to go.

And she wasn't looking at me.

"What—" Shannon gasped. "You can't— Miguel, you have to get that thing out of here. Please, you can't let—"

"Shannon, what? Who are you talking about?"

"*Her!*" The word came out as a shriek. She pointed a trembling finger at Ari.

Instinctively, I pulled Ari farther behind me, my anger turning into something far more wary. I could feel alarm ricocheting through Ari at the look in the woman's eyes.

"Miguel, she's not—" A shudder like a convulsion ran through the woman. "You don't *understand!*"

"Okay, calm down." Miguel cast a fast look to his wife.

Veronique moved to put her arm around the woman, succeeding this time. "Shannon, you're safe."

Miguel nodded. "We know about the enforcer traits. They're—" He glanced to me and Ari, something in his face like he hoped to whatever gods he believed in that the next words were true. "They're under control."

"Under control?" Shannon let out a giggle that ended in a shriek.

My skin crawled at the sound.

"You think she's under control? You think we're *safe*? They… you don't even know. She's a monster, Miguel! She'll destroy us all! She's the end of the world and death itself, and you say she's under *control?*"

"Shannon." Veronique's voice was soothing, like she was talking to a panicking child. "That's enough. You'll have a chance to talk to Miguel and tell him everything, okay? Just—"

Shannon shoved Veronique away, her face flushing splotchy red. I tensed, fighting to keep from doing something I'd maybe, *possibly* regret.

"You put her outside," the woman snapped to Miguel. "You get that thing as far from us as you can or we're dead. We're all dead, do you hear me? She's not a *person*, Miguel. You can't let her—"

"*Okay.*" Miguel looked back to us, his expression cautious. "Harvey, would you please take Ari back downstairs?"

Harvey nodded fast and hurried for the stairway.

"No," Shannon protested. "No, he shouldn't—"

"He'll be protected." Miguel glanced pointedly to two of the gun-toting people from the bunker. They retreated with us toward the steps. "See? Everything's okay."

I nudged Ari ahead of me, not taking my eyes from the woman. Shaking her head, Shannon kept insisting that Ari was a monster.

Someone closed the trapdoor behind us, sealing the sound out and leaving us in the stairwell. In silence, we returned to the first floor.

"We'll, um, we'll stay here for a few minutes," Harvey said, his gaze darting from us to the people with guns.

None of Miguel's people said a word, all of them watching Ari as if they thought she might suddenly grow fangs and claws. Her own family was silent, their expressions lost between worry and dread.

The urge to take her and leave for the ocean was overwhelming.

"Well," Baylie commented into the quiet. "Now we have crazy people. *More* of them."

I could have hugged her. "She has to be wrong."

"You'd know," Baylie agreed firmly, the words a statement of fact rather than any kind of question. "You both, you have that connection. Anything was wrong, you'd know."

"Right," Ari managed.

I glanced to her. She wasn't looking at anyone. She was so tense, I could see her hair quivering.

The silence returned, almost malicious in its awkwardness.

"So…" Maia shifted her weight. "What was that, Ari? Back in the bunker. Those things, um…"

"That's not important right now," I said.

A desperate look flashed across Maia's face. "But she… Her arms grew *spikes,* for God's sake! Ari, what did they *do* to you? What else— what else are you—"

"She's not a monster!" I snapped.

"I didn't say that! I just—"

"Please," Ari cut in. "Stop."

I couldn't tell if she was talking to Maia or me. Or both. A scowl twisted my face. It didn't matter. I was on edge and I needed to calm down.

But we should leave. We should leave and we couldn't, because Ari wouldn't want to.

Death. The end of the world. Damn it all, between Ari and Chloe I'd heard enough of that crap to last me a lifetime—any *number* of lifetimes. And meanwhile, those bastard dehaians from the judges' payroll were back, trying to start another ruanir-dehaian war.

Tension rumbled through me, a storm with nowhere to go.

"Ari," Dhanya said, her voice meticulously calm. "Were you telling us *everything* the other day? You said they tried to make you like an enforcer. What else?"

Pain twisted through Ari like a knife. She didn't look away from the floor. "They, um… the judges called me a strakirin."

"Strakirin," Dhanya repeated in the same careful tone. "Okay. And what is that?"

Ari didn't answer.

"She's sort of like a dehaian," I explained.

Worried horror spread across Maia's face. Her gaze dropped to Ari's legs and she seemed to struggle to yank it back. "So you—"

"Are you okay?" Jace demanded. "Dehaians have to stay close to the water or they die. Do we need to—"

"I'm fine."

"Dehaians don't need that so much anymore," I said. "If the judges used traits from dehaians in the past year, she wouldn't have gotten that."

The others stared at me.

Dhanya cleared her throat. "Okay, but you, um…" She seemed to work hard to find the words. "Is it just *some* dehaian traits, or… See, we found you guys by the ocean, so…"

Nausea rolled through Ari. She didn't respond.

"Best we can tell," I said, "it's all of them."

Dhanya blinked fast, as if processing the information as quickly as possible. Maia just looked sick.

Ari saw her cousin's expression. Her nausea flared into something more like anguish and she turned away. "I'll be outside."

She bolted for the door.

Jace went after her. "Ari, wait."

She didn't stop. One of the people with guns pulled the door aside for her, appearing almost perversely relieved that she was going. The rest made no move to stop her, nor to keep Jace from following. They simply turned their attention to the monitors, where I could see her fleeing across the yard.

I glanced to Baylie, who nodded. Leaving her with Maia, Dhanya, and the nervous wreck that was Harvey, I strode after Ari and Jace.

❧ 17 ☙

ARI

I rushed out into the twilight, desperate to get away from those horrible expressions.

The ones I'd known I would see.

I gulped down a breath and kept moving. It wasn't just that my body wasn't really stable anymore—that it felt like, at a moment's notice, it could become this other *thing* that wasn't ruanir or human or anything at all. It wasn't only that I could see Maia picturing that when she looked at me, see her wondering what my body turned into, wondering how much like *me* I still appeared.

It was the ocean. And my body. And the way I hadn't stopped feeling shaky since that enforcer attacked us. The way my skin didn't seem to fit right anymore. The way I could feel the sea on the other side of the large yard, the awareness stronger than it had been but different than before. I could close my eyes and spin around till I was dizzy, and I'd still know exactly in which direction it lay.

The water was calling to me, pulling at me like it had hooks dug into my skin. I could barely think with it so close, which only proved how much about me had changed.

And because of that, Maia had stared at me like…

I fought back tears. It didn't matter. I'd handle this. I'd handle all of it. I wouldn't let my body change again, and just because that woman had called me *death* didn't mean—

"Ari!" Jace shouted behind me.

I didn't turn around. The storage shed lay ahead of me. I darted inside.

Like walls between me and the water made a damn bit of difference.

I exhaled, the sound ragged. The dust and shadows of the shed closed around me and I wished I could disappear into them. That woman had to be wrong. I didn't even know what she'd *meant*, yet she still had to be wrong.

But she'd been there, part of the judges' project. She'd known *exactly* what they were going to do to me.

And she might know what they were after.

My feet stopped, leaving me beside Miguel's black truck. Of its own accord, my gaze crept up, finding the shattered rear window where the enforcer had broken through to grab me.

Footsteps thudded. "Ari, please." Jace sounded out of breath, as if he'd been running. Had I? The memory was a blur of weeds and branches and things I didn't want to feel.

Dehaians were fast. Strong.

I shivered.

"Ari…" Jace's footsteps came toward me. Beyond the shed, I could feel Noah walking toward us, his pace slower than either of ours had been.

He seemed watchful. Protective.

The reason clicked. Enforcers. He was probably keeping an eye out for them, just in case. I wished he would come in here, though. I didn't want to deal with the chance Jace would make everything that'd happened to me seem like even *more* of my fault than I knew it was already.

"Talk to me, Ari. Please. Say something."

I looked over my shoulder. "What happened?"

He blinked as if alarmed.

"I thought you cared," I said. "I thought you… you're my *brother*. I thought you'd be there for me! But instead, you stopped speaking to me. You stopped even looking at me. You just left me to…"

Jace stared at me. "Ari, I—"

"*Why*? It can't be this." My hands flailed at my body. "You didn't even know about that till now. So what? Why are you treating me like this?"

A pained sound left my brother, halfway between a scoff and a cry. He gaped at me like I'd gut-punched him, and then he turned away sharply, his hands coming up to grasp his light brown hair.

I didn't move, watching him. Outside, I could feel Noah come to a stop. He hesitated and then retreated as if giving us distance.

Jace dropped his hands from his hair. "Treating you…" he gasped. "Treating…" He whirled back to me. "Ari, this is *my fault*. All of it. Everything! What you—"

He gestured toward me, desperation on his face like he couldn't find the words to make me understand. And I didn't. Nothing he was saying made sense.

"What do you mean?"

"I agreed to this! *I* did! I could have stopped it. I could have kept this whole mess from ever happening to you, and instead I was *right there* and I argued for you to do it and I didn't—"

"Huh?"

"They hurt you." He bit off the words. "They took you away from me. I can't even touch you. Until a few hours ago, you didn't even know who I *was*, and if I'd been paying attention, if I hadn't pushed you to say yes that day, or if I'd fought harder to—"

Baffled, I moved toward him before I could stop myself. That's what he thought? Why he'd looked so angry? "Jace, you're not responsible for this."

He didn't respond, his gaze on the rough dirt floor of the shed. He was only an arm's length from me. It took effort to keep myself from reaching out to him.

"Jace, you're *not*. I was there too, remember? They lied to us both. And even if you *hadn't* been there, I would've said yes anyway."

"I should've been smarter, though. I should have been so much *fucking* smarter."

Confusion hit me all over again. "What are you talking about?"

"Mom. I should have… She wouldn't let you move out six months ago. Suddenly, after all those years of barely acknowledging we existed, she…" He appeared nauseated.

Fear bubbled through me. "What?"

"Did she tell you why she wouldn't let you leave?"

I shrugged a shoulder, still watching him. "Not really. Just… humans. Child and Family Services raising questions if I moved out before turning eighteen. Something like that."

A wry sound left him in response, filled with disgust.

But it wasn't for her, I realized. Not *only* her, at least. And it wasn't for me. This rage, all of it had never been about me.

It was for himself.

"You were important to her," he said. "That's what she told me. You were *important*. She wanted you close. And I… I should have questioned that. My God, I should have questioned that. I mean, this is *her*. She resented the hell out of us moving in after Dad died. We hadn't been more important than dryer lint for most of our lives, and now suddenly she wants to keep you nearby?" He shook his head contemptuously. "But I didn't push it. I was angry, sure, but finals were going on and life was happening and I just… I chalked it up to more of her insanity. I thought maybe she was trying to play the 'good mother' or something. Figured we'd wait till after your birthday and you'd be out anyway."

"Well, yeah, that was—"

"I was an idiot," he said flatly. "A goddamn, distracted idiot. I wasn't putting the pieces together. Wasn't even paying attention to them, because I was caught up in my own damn life when I should have been watching out for you."

"Jace, you can't blame your—"

"I saw that judge come to Mom's place last summer."

I froze.

"Engle, the one who 'helped' you. He showed up one day out of the blue, almost a year ago. I thought Mom was going to pass out from joy. But he met her in private, talked to her for like an hour. And I knew it was bizarre. I mean, she hadn't even been able to speak with their *assistants* for years, and then Judge Engle shows up personally?"

Jace scoffed, the sound cold. I didn't know what to say.

"But when he left, she was so happy. Like, *creepy* happy. I thought it was about having one of them there, but then she asked me where you were. I think you'd gone shopping with Maia or something, and when I told her that, she didn't seem too concerned, but…" He shook his head. "Dammit, I should have known. I should have known about all of it! It was right there in front of my face, the fact that they were planning something for you, and if I hadn't been so goddamn caught up in my own life, you wouldn't—"

"Jace," I protested.

"I had the power to stop this! That bitch was feeding you drugs for a *year*, and if I'd just—"

"It's not your fault!"

My heart broke for the look on his face and it was everything I could do to keep from reaching out to him. He thought he'd failed me. Failed to keep me safe, to keep me as me, and shame and guilt had been eating him alive. Everything he described all seemed like signs from *this* point of view, sure, but how could he have known that at the time? *I* hadn't. My mother had insisted I come to a Judiciary gala after not wanting to be seen near me for years—and had I thought that meant she was intending to destroy my life that night? Intending to hand me over to the judges for experimentation after exposing me to the Beast's magic? Of course not.

"You couldn't have known," I said. "Mom is *insane*. You know that; I know that. So she acted weird about me moving out. Or after seeing a judge. You remember my tenth birthday? How she refused to fly to Arizona because an assistant to an *assistant* of a judge might have been in town, so she couldn't leave Chicago? Or how—" I balked, not sure I should bring it up. "How she was after what happened with Logan? How all she could see was a chance to get in good with Judge Marseilles, so she tried to insist I go out with that bastard again? Of *course* you didn't think anything of how she acted. It just looked like more of the crazy."

He shook his head, anguish in his eyes. "I should have known she'd be capable of this, though. That she could try something like—"

"It's not your fault. I *swear* to you, it's not."

Jace looked away. "It was so... The idea that you couldn't even *remember* me..."

I wanted so badly to hug him, it was painful. "I'm sorry."

He looked back up at me fast, his eyes like stone. "It wasn't you."

I swallowed. "Or you."

His jaw muscles worked for a moment. "This thing they did. What did they call it?"

I didn't want to talk about this part. "Strakirin."

"Whatever it is, you're not a monster, okay? I don't care what that bitch thinks. You're not *death* and you're not going to be some fucking end of the world. And Maia's just scared of you getting hurt. She could've handled that better, but she doesn't think you're a monster either. I promise you."

I nodded, hoping he was right.

"Noah said it was like a dehaian?"

I hesitated. "Sort of."

Jace waited.

I turned away, drawing in on myself. "I don't really want to—"

"Ari, you are *not* a monster."

"I don't want you to imagine me looking like that."

He let out a breath. "I get that."

I pulled my gaze back to him.

"But I don't want you to be scared of me," he continued. "Or of what I might think. You're my sister, no matter what. And we're going to fix this. Somehow, we will fix *all* of this."

My head moved in a tiny nod.

"Does it hurt?" he pressed. "Being here, becoming… that. Any of it."

I searched for a response and I couldn't find one. I knew I should lie, but I didn't want to. Not to him.

"Sort of. Yeah." My voice was choked. "It, uh, the ocean's just—"

"Do you need to, like—" Jace tossed a quick glance to the storage shed door like he was ready to jump into action. "We could go to the water?"

My eyes wanted to slide toward the coast. I tensed, fighting the impulse. I wondered if Noah was picking up on this feeling too. "It… it's fine."

"What about Noah? Is he—"

"Noah's helping," I interrupted, suddenly protective. I didn't want Jace blaming him. "He's helping with all of it."

Jace was quiet for a second. "Yeah. I noticed you two seem… close."

Embarrassment flooded me. "I didn't mean— We're not, like—"

Jace held up his hands. "I wasn't saying that."

I remembered how to breathe.

"I'm glad he's helping," Jace continued. "But, Ari, please be careful. He's still the Beast. He's not—"

"He's a person too," I countered, my embarrassment quickly turning to anger. "Jace, he understands this. He knows what it's—"

I cut off. I couldn't explain to Jace why Noah understood becoming something totally different from what I'd been. Not really. Noah understood because he'd been greliaran—and then the Beast had sort of killed him.

That'd only make Jace more worried.

"I know what he is," I said instead. "He's the guy who nearly died trying to save me at the judges' lab the other day. I saw him in his other form. I… I can feel that inside my head. But I'm not afraid of him because I've also felt how scared he is that he might hurt me. That I might *get* hurt—by anyone." I hesitated. "I don't know what else we are to each other, but we are friends. I do know that."

Something twisted inside me at the words. We were probably beyond "friends," given our time in the bunker.

If I was honest, I didn't really want to be only that anyway.

I pushed the thought aside. "He's helping me. Whatever is inside him, it's changing what the judges did to me. It's letting me fight. Stay myself, no matter what the judges wanted me to become."

Jace looked away. I waited, watching him and desperately hoping he believed my words. "If there's anything I can do," he said quietly. "If you need to leave, go to the ocean, whatever, just… please. Know that I'll help too."

A pang of gratitude and heartache for my big brother twinged in my chest. I nodded. "I do."

Jace let out a breath. "I'm assuming he's out there?" He twitched his head toward the yard.

"He's giving us space."

Jace paused. "I don't mean to be such a jerk to him."

"You're not."

His brow rose and fell, his expression clearly arguing to the contrary. "Yeah, well, regardless. I only want to be sure you're okay."

I nodded again. "I am. Much as I can be."

He seemed to process the response. "We should probably get back in there. See what Miguel has to say about that… woman."

I hesitated. "You trust them?"

He gave me a curious glance.

I winced. "I remember Miguel and Veronique. I mean, I haven't thought about them in *forever*, but… I guess that's kind of the point. They vanished like three years before Dad died. They claim now that they were protecting us and maybe they were, but—" I struggled to find a way to explain. "The judges seemed trustworthy too. And Mom did what she did, and Dad was apparently some big resistance leader who *lied* to us our whole lives, and—"

I stopped, questioning my own words for a heartbeat before anger boiled up. Dad *had* lied. I hadn't really thought about it that way, seeing as how I hadn't been able to remember him for a while. But he had. Even if maybe it'd been for our own good, to keep us safe… he'd still lied to us.

Jace looked down. "Yeah."

"I saw Miguel talking to you in the hall. What was it about?"

Jace shrugged. "He wanted to know how things had been since Dad died. If we'd been okay and if we'd had any hints the judges were watching us, beyond this past year."

"Does he think the judges were behind Dad's death?"

Jace was silent for a moment. "So I'm not the only one who wondered that?"

I didn't respond.

"Miguel didn't know," Jace admitted. "He said that, from what they were able to learn, the car accident looked pretty cut and dried. But he did also say that more than a few of their people have died in the past several years, including his own brother. He's concerned."

Jace ran a hand over his hair. "I don't know if they're trustworthy. They're…" He shook his head. "I remember them too. They seemed *normal,* their weird tendency to only travel at night aside."

I made a wry noise. His lip twitched, but the expression died almost immediately.

"And I remember Dad," Jace continued. "The way he wasn't too happy about the Judiciary. He tried to hide it, toe the party line and all that, but… I could tell, even if I never really understood why." His mouth tightened. "So maybe he was this big resistance leader. Maybe Veronique and Miguel were protecting us by cutting ties before he died. The way Miguel shot that enforcer, though… I mean, *damn.* But then, I'm also alive thanks to that. So yeah, I don't know. I just think they're the best bet we have to do something about these bastards."

"The judges?"

"Whether or not they killed Dad, they *did* almost kill me. They did this to you. They used my little sister as a lab rat and it's only because our ancient enemy turned out to be a decent guy that I'm still here and you're not one of the undead. So I'm going to take any chance I've got to keep the Judiciary from hurting us again, and at the moment, that's this resistance thing."

I hesitated. "Yeah."

Jace nodded. "Yeah," he echoed. He glanced back toward the house. "But we'll still be careful. See what Miguel has to say about that woman, and if anything feels off… we'll go."

I made a noise of agreement, my gaze going to the house as

well. Jace was right—and not simply because his plan was the only one we had.

I just hoped that, if something did go wrong, getting out of here would be that simple.

Noah was waiting by the house, leaning against the rotted porch. The sunlight was nearly gone from the horizon, leaving him mostly a shadow in the deepening darkness.

"Everything alright?" he asked when we walked up to him.

"Yeah," I said.

The front door opened. Miguel stopped at the sight of us.

"What was that?" Jace asked before the man could say anything.

Miguel seemed to weigh how to respond. "Shannon was interrogated by the judges."

I heard Jace mutter a curse.

"Veronique thinks it…" Miguel's mouth tightened. "Well, she's not entirely sure. Shannon's one of the calmest people we know. War zones wouldn't fluster her. But the judges had her for nearly twenty hours. Apparently, they questioned every survivor of your escape, checking for any sign that they'd taken in magic from you." He twitched his chin to Noah. "She hadn't. No one had, from what she's told us. But the Judiciary was less than gentle about determining that."

It wasn't hard for me to remember my own brief "questioning" by the judges. To endure that for twenty *hours*…

"And the parts about Ari?" Jace pressed.

"There's no denying that the judges have some plan behind what they did to Ari," Miguel admitted, "and I hope you won't take offense to the fact that I'm going to have a few guys stick around, for our protection as much as yours. But I don't think what Shannon said should be taken literally, either. After what they put her through, Veronique and I agree she's most likely fixated on Ari as the cause of her suffering. As the 'thing'—if you'll forgive the term—that made her world fall apart." He sighed. "I have three of my people watching her. Armed, just in case."

I felt sick.

"We'll keep her upstairs till we can figure out more," Miguel finished, "and we can move some cots—"

He stopped, looking beyond me. I turned to see headlights cutting through the trees, racing toward us. Miguel moved past us down the steps, not taking his eyes from the approaching lights, and his hand drifted toward his back as if reaching for a weapon.

Which was probably what he was doing.

My forearms stung. Noah came closer to my side, putting a hand to my back as if to calm me and protect me at the same time. From the corner of my eye, I saw a few more people emerge from the house, rifles in hand and their eyes on the road.

A white car bounded onto the property. It skidded to a stop, the headlights blocking our view of the person inside. The door opened.

Willa climbed out.

She looked like hell. Her red ponytail was disheveled and appeared as if it'd been tied back blindly. Her arm bore a bandage that'd been torn from her own t-shirt. Blood showed through the fabric. Her cheek was swollen as if she'd been punched.

And her expression was filled with rage.

"What happened?" Miguel called, striding toward her.

"They killed my grandmother, that's what happened! That *bastard* just—"

She cut off, seething, and then she caught sight of Noah. I couldn't read the reactions that flashed over her face.

Miguel didn't seem to have that trouble. "Who told you about him?"

She glanced to Miguel. "You *knew?*"

"Learned of it right after you left the mess hall."

She stared like she couldn't decide what to say first.

The door behind me opened again. Several people rushed past, one of them carrying a first aid kit. Maia, Dhanya, and Baylie trailed them out, watching Willa and us warily.

"Come on." Miguel looped one of her arms over his shoulder and helped her back to the porch stairs. Easing her down carefully, he nodded for another man to start removing the makeshift bandage from her arm. "So who was it that came to the house? What judge?"

Willa hissed between her teeth when the fabric pulled away, revealing a deep gouge along the side of her bicep. "None. Enforcers and that slimy bastard Logan Marseilles."

My blood froze.

"Wait, *he's* involved in this?" Jace demanded.

Noah looked from them to me, clearly picking up on my reaction. "Who?"

I didn't know what to say. My body felt like it had been dropped into ice water, like I was shivering from a cold that was spreading from the inside out. This was bad. *So* bad. I couldn't have Logan after me. The enforcers and the judges and the whole damn world were horrible enough, but to have *Logan* out there, trying to be the one who captured me for them…

"Ari?" Noah pressed. "Who is—"

I spun away, my heart racing. Logan wouldn't find me. And if he did, I—

Something new shivered through me, cold and dark and carrying a whole new level of terror.

If Logan tried to touch me, I'd have something new I could do about that.

"*Ari*? Who the hell is this person?"

Jace made a furious sound. "Logan Marseilles is the arrogant son of a bitch who tried to *rape* Ari about a year ago."

My stomach clenched. Why did he have to tell them—

A choked noise left Maia and, from the corner of my eye, I could see Dhanya staring at me, her mouth working like she couldn't find the words she wanted to say. But everything about Noah went still. Utterly still beyond anything he'd ever done. I couldn't tell what I was feeling from him. Cold like deep space, maybe.

And equally as deadly.

"He didn't," I pointed out. "I stopped him."

Noah didn't reply.

Jace turned to Willa. "That bastard is working with the judges now?"

"He's running a group of enforcers for them. Seems the Judiciary put him in charge of finding your sister and the rest of you." Willa took a ragged breath, which cut off sharply when the guy beside her began wrapping her wound. "His mother was in that warehouse the Beast destroyed. She didn't make it out."

I balled a fist against my middle, fighting a surge of nausea. Logan was close to his mother, judge or not. I knew that. Everyone knew that. It'd always struck me as creepy somehow. But he loved the power being the son of a judge gave him. He enjoyed the way it made ruanir girls clamor for his attention, in case it'd gain them favor with his mom too.

And now we'd killed her.

"So he's even more psychotic than he was to begin with," Jace filled in.

Willa scoffed dryly, like the two of them were having the same thought.

"Did they know Ari was there?" Miguel asked.

"They knew something," Willa said. "When they first showed up, they made some pretense about traveling around to warn ruanir about the Beast's return, which they had to know we'd think was bullshit. But they didn't even get five feet from the door before Logan sent those snake bastards back in."

Miguel grimaced.

"They poisoned her," Willa continued, her voice becoming tight. "That pompous ass sauntered back inside and had them start poisoning my grandmother to force me to talk." She took a shaky breath, her resolve and anger starting to fracture. "She… The house was my fault. She told me to do it. She knew she wouldn't make it, but…"

"You did what you had to do," Miguel said quietly.

Willa nodded like she was hanging onto the words.

"Come on," Miguel continued, tossing a quick look to the guy bandaging Willa's injuries. "Veronique and Declan have enough energy between them to help you get charged back up a bit, and we'll work on getting the seawater converters going in the morning. Till then, get some rest."

Willa nodded. Bracing herself on the rough wooden steps, she pushed back to her feet and headed inside.

"She's like Declan and Veronique?" Jace asked. "She can use that new form of ocean magic?"

Miguel nodded. "We all hope to, eventually."

I saw Maia shift her weight, discomfort flashing over her face.

"You all should get some rest too," Miguel continued. "It's getting too dark and we can't risk being detected by running the lights out here. We'll pick back up in the morning."

I didn't move, uncertain what to do. I didn't want to be upstairs with that woman, the one who had called me *death*.

Miguel seemed to notice my hesitation. "I'll have someone move some cots down to the first floor for you all. There's a side room that should give you some privacy."

He walked toward the door. Maia and the others stepped aside to let him pass.

"You, uh… you okay?" Baylie asked, her tone somehow including me and Noah both.

I could feel Noah watching me. I could feel the questions starting to boil under that cold, weird sensation inside him. But I couldn't bring myself to look at him. At any of them. I didn't want to talk about Logan or anything at all. Now that Miguel had headed inside and the distraction of the past few moments was over, the questions were bound to come.

I was so sick of questions. Always questions, as if my life was a mess that could never be sorted out. And that wasn't all. The fishhook-feeling of the ocean pulling at my body and mind was coming back too. Tenfold.

Without a word, I hurried after Miguel.

Nothing got better as the night went on. Noah watched me in silence. The others gave up on making small talk and went to bed. The house turned into an abyss of darkness.

In a small room on the first floor, the others were asleep on cots and narrow mattresses. Beneath a patchwork blanket as far away from them—and the door—as I could get, I lay with my eyes wide open and my body aching with the feeling of fishhooks burrowing into my bones. My chest shook with the pain of it and my fingers curled into the rough army mattress beneath me like I was trying to hold myself to the thing. And maybe I was. Every muscle screamed with the urge to bolt for the front door right now. My skin burned and itched with the urge to change. The compulsion to run for the water dragged at me like a hundred pounds of weight and gravity itself, pulling down my resolve to stay, to hold onto human form, to keep away from the ocean that could swallow me whole.

A twist of discomfort rose from the dark swirl of Noah's presence in my mind. He had to be feeling this. He'd hardly said a word all evening, but surely he could feel this.

I didn't want to deal with what I was picking up from him.

My eyes squeezed shut. It hadn't changed in hours, that swirling morass of *something* coming from him. He'd gone cold like the arctic, and beneath the ice was a darkness like that day in the judges' lab. The Beast, churning with unspeakable power held only temporarily at bay.

If I hadn't been in so much pain, it would have been vaguely terrifying.

A shudder rippled through my muscles and a choked gasp escaped me. I clamped my mouth shut, fighting to hold back any sound that might wake the others sleeping nearby.

"Ari?"

My breath caught at Jace's whisper. Blankets rustled a few feet away from me.

"Ari, was that you?"

I trembled.

"Are you okay?" Jace pressed.

"Fine," I choked out.

He paused. "What's going on?"

Speaking was difficult. The words kept wanting to turn into a sob.

Or maybe a scream.

"Nothing," I managed.

I felt Noah move from where he sat beside the door. He didn't make a sound. Anger built up fast in me, pushing at him. I didn't want him disagreeing with me in front of Jace.

He stopped, and the darkness and God knew what else inside him took on a stillness, like everything had been put on pause though none of it had gone away. "It's only going to get worse," he told me, his words barely audible.

Jace moved, the blankets rustling again. "What is?"

"I'm fine," I snarled in a whisper.

Noah was silent for a heartbeat. "This hurts, Ari."

Guilt tangled through me, hot and agonizing.

"She's feeling the pull of the water," Noah said to Jace. "The urge to change shape too. Dehaians can't stay in human form forever. They need to be in their other form as well."

I made a choked noise, furious and begging him to stop all at the same time.

"Ari," Jace began, "you should have said—"

"It'll pass," I insisted. "I'm fine."

Noah bent down beside me and his hand came to rest on my shoulder. I wanted to pull away, but it'd only bring me dangerously close to Jace.

"No, it won't," Noah said gently. "And no, you're not."

I shook my head.

"Ari," he urged.

"I'm fine."

His lips brushed my forehead. "Let me help you."

I closed my eyes, a desperate protest trapped inside me. Maybe a cry. I didn't want to be this. To become this. Not again.

His hands slipped under me. The ground fell away as he scooped me and the blanket into his arms and then stood up like I weighed nothing.

Maybe to him I did.

"Get the door?" he whispered to Jace.

I heard Jace pass us. A soft click sounded to my left, and then a bluish light paled the darkness when he opened the door. Jace slipped into the next room and silently, Noah followed.

The two women on watch glanced over to us. Images of the area around the house showed on the screens beside them.

"Everything's okay," Jace assured them immediately. "She just needs to get some air."

The women didn't respond. Eyeing us warily, one of them headed toward the exit. Quickly, she punched a code into the small keypad on the wall and then pulled the door aside.

Cool air burned my skin, the breeze heavy with salt, and in Noah's arms, I writhed. I didn't want to do this. I didn't *need* to do this. I could wait this out. It'd pass; I was certain of it.

"Shh," Noah whispered.

I bit my lip, realizing I must have made a sound.

Jace's footsteps paused on the porch. "She okay?"

"Yeah."

Noah was lying.

I squeezed my eyes shut. I didn't care what Noah thought. I was fine. Really.

"This way," Noah continued.

Jace's shoes thudded on the porch steps and then went silent when we reached the overgrown yard. Not too far away, I could hear water rushing up against the shore beyond the bluffs.

Shudders rumbled through me. "We shouldn't," I whispered to Noah. "I'll be fine. Just take me back inside."

He didn't respond.

"Noah, please. What if this—" I swallowed hard. "What if it makes it happen again? The thing, in the lab. In the truck. What if this brings it back?"

He shifted me in his arms. I could feel us moving down more stairs.

The sound of the ocean grew louder.

"Please," I begged.

Our descent stopped.

"I'll be with you," Noah whispered. "I won't leave you. I promise."

Gravel crunched briefly. Jace had reached the bottom of the steps. Noah started moving again. His feet didn't make a sound.

"So what now?" Jace asked tensely.

"Open your eyes, Ari," Noah said.

I shook my head. I could feel the ocean. Everything in my body screamed to shove Noah aside, to scramble for the water right now.

But I'd lose myself. I'd become that *thing* again.

My fingers dug into his shoulder.

"Ari, please," Jace urged.

His voice was so pained, it was frightening. I looked over to him. By the base of the stairs, he gripped the banister. His gaze darted from me to the water.

A breath escaped me. This was so dangerous for him, being this close to the ocean and its magic.

He started toward me.

"No!" I gasped.

Jace stopped.

"Please, Jace. Go back. We can all go back. I don't need to—"

"Yes, you do," my brother interrupted, his voice tight.

I shivered. My head shook of its own accord. "But I don't want to—"

"You'll be okay." He glanced to Noah like he was ordering him not to make him a liar.

"Take the blanket," Noah said rather than respond. "She'll need it when we get back."

I couldn't keep myself from whimpering in pain when Jace reached over and pulled the blanket away. The air hurt. Everything hurt.

Without a word, Noah turned. The smell of salt grew stronger. Droplets splashed me, burning my skin, while he walked deeper into the tide.

"No," I begged. "Please."

He lowered me into the water. The cold waves swallowed me and a surge of electricity came with them.

I shrieked, only to choke when the water filled my mouth.

I thrashed in Noah's grasp, fighting desperately to break free while magic scorched through my skin and muscles and bones, devouring me alive. I couldn't stop it. Couldn't control it. My body convulsed and my legs locked together, the skin merging, the bones shifting.

But the pain faded. The fishhooks changed, easing a bit yet still trying to draw me somewhere. The pressure inside melted away, though, turning into a disturbing sort of calm like I'd given my body what it needed. Like in some terrifying way, this was more *right* than my other form. All that was left was to swim toward the feeling still tugging at me.

I gritted my teeth against the inexplicable pull, fighting to stay where I was. However far into the ocean I was right now was more than far enough. I didn't need to go anywhere. But that wasn't the only thing.

With a frantic intensity, I summoned up memories of Jace. My dad. Maia and Dhanya and Baylie too.

They were all there.

My chest rose and fell in ragged gasps. I was okay. I was still myself—inside, anyway. The only thing that'd changed was my body. Well, my body and that compulsion to keep swimming toward who-knew-what, though really, even that wasn't as strong as it had been on land.

And Noah's arms were still around me.

I opened my eyes. The water was a dim twilight, the shadows lessened only by the faint glow of moonlight rippling beyond the waves rolling above our heads. He'd taken us deeper beneath the sea even as my body changed.

Noah reached up and brushed the faintly glowing strands of my floating hair away from my face. "You okay?" he asked.

I couldn't bring myself to meet his eyes. I knew what I looked like now. Green scales. A tail like an eel.

Nothing like a person.

I glanced to the ocean's surface. We weren't far from air, though. If I changed here, I'd probably be okay. Except for ending up naked, anyway.

Maybe I could control that better this time around.

I bit my lip, concentrating.

"Ari?" Noah pressed.

Shivers ran through my body, nowhere near as painful as last time. Nowhere even close. The scales disappeared, retreating until they were only a green swimsuit covering my body. My legs returned.

And then darkness did too.

I blinked fast, looking around. Everything was darker. I could barely see Noah in the water.

And meanwhile, my lungs were starting to demand oxygen.

I kicked for the waves above us. Noah released me and then followed immediately.

My head broke past the surface. Gratefully, I gulped down a lungful of air and then looked around.

We weren't *that* far from shore. The moonlight cast a silver sheen on the pale shape of the lighthouse. The bluffs were a mix of deep shadows and rough rocks that glistened with a coating of ocean mist.

I couldn't see Jace, but I could make out the lumpy shape of the blanket folded on the bottom step of the staircase. I let out a breath, relieved. He must have headed back inside, since it was all *kinds* of unsafe, him being this close to the water.

Kicking hard, I swam toward the shore. My legs wobbled when I reached the sand and gravel of the beach. Noah steadied me quickly.

A blush burned my cheeks. His hands felt good on my skin, warm and soothing and, yeah, intimate. Now that the pain and the adrenaline and the overriding terror that I'd lose myself were gone… I realized he'd been touching my bare skin for a while now.

And I didn't really want him to let me go.

I paused, my gaze skirting around briefly before managing the journey up to meet his own.

"You okay?" he asked.

I nodded.

The corner of his mouth rose in a small smile, but a heartbeat later, a weird sort of discomfort flickered through his expression.

He looked away, something about him going cold again.

"What?" I asked.

He shook his head. Dropping his hands from me, he turned and crossed the beach to the stairway.

I followed him. "Noah? What is it?"

He picked up the blanket and wrapped it around me without a word.

"*Noah.*"

"That guy. Logan."

Understanding hit me. Right. That.

I didn't want to talk about that.

He felt my uneasiness. The storm inside him became colder still and he moved away, putting a few steps of distance between us.

"Nothing happened," I insisted to him.

Noah glanced back at me and I could just read it, that look in his eyes. He heard the words. He also felt the way I reassured myself with them.

"That bastard tried to rape you."

"But he *didn't*."

Noah snarled wordlessly, turning away again.

I stared at him. "Why are you—" A new thought hit me and my blood went cold. A wave of dread coursed through my body. "Does this… does this *change* something about me for you?" I pushed the question out. "About us? Is that it? Are you—"

He whirled back. "*What?*"

"Does this change something?" I bit off the words, my heart clenching in my chest. "I mean, what do you think? That I 'let' him almost rape me? That I 'let' him shove me down on his couch, grab at my clothes, ignore my shouts for him to stop? That I led him on? You think I had a part in this? Is that what you're—"

Noah was across the beach in a heartbeat, his hands grabbing my shoulders as if to stop my words, stop me, stop everything. For a moment, I stared at him, my chest rising and falling with rapid breaths while ice cold blood rushed in my ears.

"No." His green eyes burned down at me like emeralds lit by fire. "I don't."

I trembled. "Then what?"

He was silent, almost as if searching for a way to explain, and then he asked, "Who the hell said that to you?"

I hesitated. "My mother. She said I didn't understand what guys did when they liked a girl. And that if I had a problem, I shouldn't have let him think I wanted him to do that in the first place. She said I led him on and should apologize, and then make it up to him by going on another date."

Noah's hands trembled where they gripped my shoulders. He squeezed his eyes shut, rage boiling inside him like a volcano about to explode.

"And do you *believe* that?" he asked, his voice low.

I managed a scoff. "No."

He looked at me.

"I don't. I..." I turned my face away. I didn't know how to explain. "It wasn't my fault, what he tried. I know that. And he didn't get to, so—"

"Not the point."

My gaze snapped back to him. "It is the point."

He was silent.

I stared at him, trying to find the words. "Logan is a bastard, okay? He's a sick, twisted *psychopath*. And he wanted to do that to me. Hurt me like that. And I'm not saying that's not horrible. I'm not saying that, because he didn't get away with it, that makes everything somehow okay, or that the fact I fought him off makes me somehow... *better* than any other girl he could've done that to. I'm not saying that. Not even close. And I wish to *God* he was locked up for being the monster that he is."

I drew a breath. "But the fact he didn't get to do that to me *is* my point, because I was the one who stopped him. His mother wouldn't have cared if he got away with it, Noah. She wouldn't have batted an eye. His servants heard me shouting, heard everything from *right outside* that room, and they didn't lift a finger to stop him. And my mother? She would have preferred I let him because maybe then he would've wanted to see me again." My insides trembled with old rage and a pain that never seemed to go away. "But I stopped him. Maybe Logan isn't in jail or dead or out of favor with the Judiciary for being a wannabe-rapist pig, but he is the bastard who didn't get to do that to me. And that *matters*."

Noah was quiet for a long moment before he gave a tight nod. I knew he believed me. Even agreed. But the rage wasn't gone.

"What is it?" I asked.

His jaw muscles jumped. "Come back to the ocean with me."

I recoiled. "What?"

"Come back. Let me take you away from this. We can go to Yvaria. Farther, even. Head for the coast of China or the Mediterranean. There are these cave formations I found off the coast of Italy that—"

I yanked away from him, stumbling back. "Are you crazy? I'm not… I'm not *ever* going in the ocean again, not if I can help it."

"But—"

"No!" I stared at him. "I'm not dehaian, Noah! I'm not even this. I'm a ruanir and a normal girl and I'm not—"

"These people want to kill you, Ari!"

My mouth moved, wordless.

"They want your body alive and for everything else you are to be dead." Noah's voice was choked. "And now they've sent the bastard who tried to… who ever laid a goddamn *hand* on you to…"

He turned away, his fists clenching so tightly I could see the veins standing out on his arms.

A short breath left me. Waves of rage and pain buffeted me, like the entire storm inside him was aching to roar out its fury across the sky.

And for me. Because someone, anyone, might have hurt me.

I walked toward him, my bare feet sinking into the cool sand. I reached up, resting my fingertips on his shoulder. A shudder went through him like it came from the core of the earth.

"When I think of something happening to you…" he said quietly. "Of someone hurting you… doing that to you…"

He shook his head and then looked back at me. Questions in his eyes, he extended a hand, silently offering.

I stepped closer. He engulfed me in an embrace.

"I'm sorry." His hand stroked my wet hair. "I'm not upset at you. I didn't mean to make you think I was."

I nodded. "I know."

His arms wrapped around me tighter. He kissed the top of my head and then rested his cheek there, never letting me go.

I closed my eyes, hurt draining away while I breathed in the smell of him. Warm like the sand beneath the sun. Salt like the ocean waves. Cool like the scent of the earth after rain.

It was so him.

For a long moment, the faint drum of his heartbeat and the waves rushing into the shore behind me were the only sounds.

"I can't go back there, Noah," I whispered. "I'm sorry. I can't leave my family when maybe I could protect them instead."

Resignation spread through him. He'd known that would be my answer. I was sure of it.

"Just promise me," he said. "If it gets to the point where they'll be safer without us, then please… please let me take you somewhere you'll be—"

Glass shattered atop the bluff. I looked up, startled, only to find that the cliff blocked my view. Shouts rang out above us.

Then gunfire did too.

"Stay here," Noah ordered me.

He raced up the steps so quickly, I wasn't sure he was entirely hanging onto human form. Alarm shot through him when he reached the top of the stairs, followed by confusion. He ran toward the lighthouse.

"Ari!" I heard Maia call. "Ari, where—"

Her voice cut off.

"Maia!" I shed the blanket from my shoulders and tore up the steps, only to slam to a halt when I came to the top.

The lighthouse was on fire.

I stared in horror. The lantern room was an inferno. Flames poured up from it, turning the yard into a nightmare of orange light and ghastly shadows.

And people on the ground.

I raced toward them, scanning the yard wildly. "Maia!"

"Over here!"

I turned, spotting her by the house. Dhanya and Jace were with her. Baylie too. Soldiers ran past them, racing for the blaze, while several others were scanning the property, weapons at the ready to defend against anything coming our way.

I couldn't see Noah.

"What happened?" I cried, rushing over to my family.

"Don't know," Dhanya replied. "One minute we were sleeping and the next all hell broke—"

"Help!"

I spun toward the lighthouse. Noah was coming out the door and two people were with him, both with their arms over his shoulders for support. Miguel followed, carrying Veronique.

"Somebody help us!" Miguel shouted.

My heart climbed my throat. Veronique wasn't moving.

Declan rushed from a cluster of people several yards away. He had a red bag marked with a first aid cross slung over his shoulder. "Set her down, set her down."

Miguel lowered his wife to the grass.

Declan kneeled beside her, feeling quickly for her pulse, and then moving on to see if she was breathing. "Put them over there, Beast." He motioned sharply at Noah. "Takashi! Check them!"

Another guy rushed from the group, only to hesitate when he spotted Noah.

"Now, dammit!" Declan barked without looking away from Veronique.

The man continued over and nervously helped Noah lower the people to the ground.

"What the hell happened?" Declan demanded of Miguel.

"Not sure." Miguel didn't take his eyes from his wife. "She was up early trying to get the ocean magic converters started to help Willa. It shouldn't have caused any—"

Veronique coughed hard, lurching on the ground. Miguel moved fast to help her when she attempted to sit up. She waved him off, shaking her head as if to assure him she was okay despite still coughing.

"Careful," Declan ordered. "Don't—"

A shout cut him off, and the sound was followed by screams. I looked back.

Someone was standing on the upper floor of the lighthouse, their body silhouetted by flames. For an endless moment, they were motionless on the ledge.

And then they jumped.

"Oh my God!" Maia cried.

The person slammed down into a crouch on the ground and then they were rising again. Moving again.

Racing straight at me.

I backpedaled, horrified. It was Shannon. She charged across the ash-coated grass, running faster than should have been possible. Her gaze was locked on me, but her eyes were unlike anything I'd ever seen. Wild. Inhuman.

And she had a gun.

Panic hit me, and then ice did too, shooting through my veins in a torrent of frigid calm. Seconds became years. Became centuries. I could stop this.

I would.

Poison surged inside me like a flood utterly under my control. Green stains raced over my skin. Translucent spikes rushed from my forearms to glisten in the firelight.

I ran at her.

She grinned, never taking her eyes from mine. And the sight was ghastly. Splinters of yellow and black fragmented the white, like her eyes had been turned into a kaleidoscope from hell. Swiftly, her hand swung the weapon up.

But she didn't point the gun at me.

Horror painted itself across Maia's face in slow motion. I saw Dhanya reaching for her. Baylie, scrambling to shove my cousin out of the way.

And then Shannon fired.

Baylie stumbled. Noah cried out and agony flooded our connection. It staggered me, fracturing my control, and sent the world shuddering back into horrific high speed.

Maia grabbed Baylie as she collapsed.

Shannon ignored them. She flung the gun to the ground and then lunged. Her hands landed on my temples, her fingers digging into my scalp.

Ice slammed into my world, joining with the poison already inside me and crashing through me a thousand times stronger than before. My breathing stopped. My heart froze. The teetering scale of control inside my mind collapsed under the weight of the magic. Nothing could stop the destruction this time.

Cracks spread through my insides, through my mind, deep into my core. Something was dying. Something was being destroyed.

Like glass, my connection to Noah shattered.

The world vanished down a long tunnel, everything paralyzed and frozen in time. My mind was falling with it, leaving my body. In desperation, I clawed at the walls of darkness. At the light. At anything to cling onto. Anything to keep from dying completely.

The world stopped receding. In the darkness, I hung, trapped in my own mind like a gnat in mud.

I couldn't control anything. Couldn't move.

The darkness swelled up like a living thing all around me. It knew I was here. It pressed down on me. It wouldn't give me anywhere to hide.

And… and that was right.

I strained against the thought, desperate to hang on, but my will to fight was leaching out at the whispering lullaby of the cold. At the pleasure it promised, so simple. So pure. I knew that joy now. Knew the clarity of having one purpose. One meaning to my existence. And I wanted that, really. It would be so easy. All I had to do was let go. Stop fighting. Surrender to—

Gunshots shattered the stillness. Shannon staggered, her fingers clutching at me and jarring the darkness. Her eyes went wide and she choked, blood spurting from her mouth to splash on my cheek, my chest.

I pushed her aside.

Miguel stood beyond her, his handgun raised. Alarm filled his eyes.

"Ari!" Noah shouted. He flew at me, abandoning human form completely for the sake of speed. Shifting back fast, he grabbed my arms.

A shiver ran through me, cold but quivering with ecstasy. I wanted that too. The pleasure of the kill was a hundred times what it had been before.

Noah cried out with pain, his hands falling from me while he collapsed to the ground.

My gaze dropped to him. Poison was ripping through him, invisible for the moment, but lethal nonetheless. I could feel the magic in me, fully transformed at last. It was something stronger than it had been. More powerful, like a chemical mixture that'd needed only a sufficient amount of one vital ingredient to turn it truly deadly.

And I'd been meant to do that to him. Hurting the Beast—*killing* the Beast—was part of my purpose. A final line of defense against the creature I was meant to draw energy from, in case it tried to do anything about my masters' plans.

Something screamed in the back of my mind.

I swatted it aside. That tiny voice didn't matter anymore. My eyes lifted from the Beast. His body was thrashing out the final moments of his existence. It wouldn't be long now till he was dead. My focus landed on Jace. He was staring at me. I moved my attention to Maia, to Dhanya, both of them crouched around Baylie. Beyond them was Miguel and all his people, including his wife.

I knew what I had to do next.

Guns swung toward me. My muscles tensed, ready to race past the weapons and kill everyone there. I could feel the strength for it in me. Feel the magic pouring like black oil through my veins.

But that wasn't the only thing.

My head turned, my eyes not leaving the others. The ocean called me, but it wasn't just the water. Something else was out there too, somewhere farther along the coast.

The answer clicked. My masters. They were commanding me to return; they had been this whole time.

I wasn't only drawn to the sea. I'd never been *only* drawn to the sea.

The distant gnat whimpered in horror at the realization.

My face twitched at the tiny sound in the back of my mind, but it stopped quickly, switching to begging that I go. That I leave the others alive and follow the command, if only to avoid getting shot.

They would be so simple to kill. It would feel so good.

But my masters were calling. I had to obey.

My body spun. My feet flashed over the ground. Bullets cut through the air at my back, but I'd already leapt over the side of the bluff. The air whistled in my ears and then my feet slammed into the gravel and the sand, the impact nothing against the magic and power flowing through my bones.

I shoved up from the ground, the magic to change my shape

already racing through my body. Without a backward glance, I dove into the water.

❧ 18 ❧

NOAH

I was burning.

Pain shredded my world, pouring in from Baylie. From the gaping, ragged wound that had been my connection to Ari.

From poison.

My body lurched on the ground. Instinctively, I curled tight into a ball, wracked with agony. The poison sliced and slashed through the storm inside me like a white-hot knife, too strong, too powerful. It wasn't like what I'd taken from Ari before. I couldn't get a handle on it, couldn't stop it from cutting at me before it'd slip from my grasp again.

But Baylie. Ari. They—

The connection to Baylie shuddered. My eyes flew open, finding her on the ground a dozen yards away from me. No. Oh sweet God no, this wasn't happening.

My fingers dug into the grass, dragging me to my feet. Staggering upright, I stumbled toward her.

The bullet had torn into her chest near her shoulder, and her shirt was soaked with blood. The dirt was red around her. Maia was there, pressing her hands to the wound.

Baylie gasped and I cringed. I could feel the pain as much as see it on her face. I crumpled down at her side. I had to help her.

I didn't know what to do.

"Move!" Miguel ordered.

Dhanya scrambled away as Declan dropped down beside us. He had the first aid kit. Bandages. Supplies. Behind him, Veronique was standing, supported by others, and watching us as well.

The world blurred, my vision waffling between the broad senses of the Beast and localized human form.

"You'll be okay," Declan said to Baylie, the words more an order than a reassurance. "Keep breathing."

"Hospital," I gasped. "Have to get her to—"

The pain grew stronger. I staggered, my eyes going black and the dark shapes of storm clouds ghosting through my skin.

Declan tensed at the sight. "Infirmary here is her best chance. Takashi!"

The man who'd helped me with the others hurried forward. At Declan's sharp motion, he moved to assist with lifting Baylie off the ground.

They carried her toward one of the single-story buildings on the outskirts of the property.

I couldn't move to follow them. My legs buckled and I felt my human form falter, felt my Beast side snarling with pain and rage. There was an invader inside me. A toxin. Some disgusting, corrupt filth that those sons of bitches had put inside

Ari and it—

"Noah!"

Jace was nearby, with Miguel a few feet beyond him. I turned my head toward them, the motion jerky and hard to control. I wanted to lose this form. I wanted to destroy everything around me, if only to make the pain—

"You have to save Ari," Jace insisted. "You can't let her—"

A snarl left me, greliaran or Beast I didn't know. Baylie was dying. Everything hurt so much.

"Noah," Jace pressed.

He came closer. He was a damn fool.

"I'll protect your sister," Jace promised, crouching down beside me. "I swear to you on my *life*, I will watch out for Baylie. Just save Ari. Please."

My gaze snapped toward him.

He was scared, I could tell. But he didn't move away. Behind him, Miguel stared at us both.

I twitched my head in a nod.

And then I let my human form disappear.

I raced upward, a flood of storm clouds and lightning ripping into the night sky. I saw Jace and Miguel stumble back, saw everyone else scramble for cover, and then the world opened up below me.

Hillsides. Roads. Houses like stars in the darkness on one side and endless ocean on the other.

Lightning slashed through the black clouds of my form. I strained to keep it from hitting the ground. I couldn't stop it.

But I didn't want to make the entire countryside burn too.

The pain grew worse. If I'd still been human, I would've been screaming. The atmosphere churned around me, stirred by the magic ripping through the air. Winds picked up, whipping at the trees, and it took everything I had to keep from blasting the ground below.

A familiar feeling threaded through the poison.

Desperate, I latched onto it. The toxin shredding through me was new, but a similarity to what I'd taken from Ari before *did* exist. Something from her. Something *of* her. A trace of her essence amid the magic, like a vaccine against a plague.

And that was enough.

I snarled and thunder answered. Ocean magic flooded into me, drawn from the water below, while the winds thrashed the sea into white-crested waves. The energy swept through me, hunting for the sense of Ari, and then twisting it against the poison like a weapon. The venom fought back, snapping and tangling like a viper, but it was losing now. Weaker now. Ari's essence inside me was defeating it. The toxin lessened with every passing second until slowly, finally, the agony melted into an ache.

I struggled to rein my magic back in. It felt good, though. I hated that it felt *this* good, letting my abilities out, like stretching a limb that'd been bound up for so long.

Shudders wracked me, but the lightning and the winds died. The black clouds began to fade. From my place in the clearing sky, I scanned the terrain. No fires, barring the one at the lighthouse. No change, except for however much I'd scared everyone for miles around.

And as for Baylie…

My focus narrowed on the lighthouse, so tiny and distant in the darkness below me. The connection was still there. She was in pain, but less now.

And Ari…

I turned my attention to the west. She'd run for the sea. She'd taken off faster than any dehaian I'd ever seen.

But I couldn't find her. Couldn't feel her at all. The connection was gone and what ripped through her in the moments before it shattered—

Desperation surged in me. It didn't matter. She *couldn't* be gone. Not like the judges wanted, and not like this either. I wouldn't let her be.

I raced downward, hoping I still had time. My body condensed into human form so quickly, the people guarding the yard shouted.

Miguel was bending over Shannon. She was still alive.

Barely.

"Where is she?" I demanded, my words more growl than speech. Everything still ached, my eyes were pitch black, and my skin wasn't anything approaching normal.

But this was the closest to human that I could come.

Miguel went rigid with tension when I crouched down beside the woman. Shannon choked. She didn't have long.

I shuddered, rage pounding through me. She'd shot Baylie, poisoned Ari, and turned her into this *thing*. She'd called Ari *death,* when the whole time—

"Couldn't stop…" Shannon gasped. Blood frothed around

her mouth. Her eyes rolled toward Miguel. "Tried to fight them. Tried to…"

She shuddered hard.

"Dammit, Shannon," Miguel muttered. "I'm so sorry."

She shook her head. "Don't want to live like…" She managed a breath. "They left me… half-alive. Couldn't tell you… Had to obey." She choked. "Going to do this to all of us, Miguel. Have to stop them. But she… I was wrong. She's the… the key. I felt it, when I…" She coughed. "Remember that. Remember or they'll destroy us all."

"The key?" Miguel repeated.

"Where did she *go*?" I snarled.

"Don't know. Out there, somewhere. Masters calling her… us." Shannon's face tightened like she was fighting something beyond the pain. "I didn't want to. They ordered… trigger her. Finish procedure. Send them word… where to find you all here." Her shaking grew worse. "So sorry, Miguel. For everything. I'm so—"

Shannon lurched, her eyes squeezing shut. Her shaking continued for a moment and then eased into nothing.

Her body stilled completely.

Miguel cursed. I ignored him, looking toward the ocean. We were burning time.

I moved to leave.

"Beast."

I turned toward Miguel, seething.

"Noah," he amended. "Your… your *sister?*"

"If you hurt her…"

Confusion flashed over Miguel's face and then vanished just as quickly. "We won't, I promise you. But you heard Shannon. They know where we are. We have to get out of here the moment Baylie is stable. You find Ari, you come meet us. Inland. Old industrial complex outside Staghorn Hills, Arizona. Look for the cannon-shaped weathervane. You got that?"

I hesitated. He wanted me to come find them?

Pushing my incredulity away, I nodded. "Yeah."

My human form vanished and I raced for the water. If I had my way, Ari would be found before Miguel's people even had the chance to leave.

I wasn't losing her, not to this. Not to anything.

Not ever.

19

LOGAN

The last-minute diversion from our target had been frustrating, but what I found at our new destination made my annoyance disappear immediately.

I grinned, watching Ari float in the cube-like tank they'd arranged for her, down in this basement of an old warehouse on the outskirts of San Francisco. She'd swam here, they told me, obedient to the compulsion they'd placed inside her. Some kind of psychic homing beacon, like a mangled version of the dehaians' compulsion to find the sea.

I tapped the side of her tank, making a dull thunk sound come from the thick glass. Her yellow, snake-like gaze slid over to me.

"Mister Marseilles."

I tucked my hand away smoothly and glanced back. Judge Engle regarded me from the opposite side of the room.

"Yes, sir." I walked toward him.

"I've received word of your performance these past several days from the enforcers."

I paused. Those bastards had been *reporting* on me?

"Indeed, sir?" I made certain I sounded only politely curi-ous, as if I'd expected that all along. But if that Nazi freak, Hans, had said anything negative to the Judiciary…

"We are well pleased."

I let a trace of relief show. Only enough to appear as if I'd been hopeful I'd done my best.

Rather than damn well convinced of it and ready to annihi-late anyone who claimed differently.

Judge Engle glanced to the side. Around the room, lab atten-dants were keeping an eye on the machines that monitored the little zombie that was Ari, while enforcers stood guard in case anything went wrong. From the chatter around me, I'd gath-ered they were planning to start testing her soon to see what this monster they'd made was capable of.

"If you would come with me?" the judge prompted.

I followed him. It wasn't like there was another option.

"We are assigning you to another project," Judge Engle said. "This is not a demotion from your journeyman status, but rather an elevation of it. By taking part in this, you will become significantly more important to the Judiciary." He paused. "Invaluable, even."

Wait, what?

"That's rewarding to hear, sir," I said, being certain to sound grateful but controlled. "How may I be of assistance?"

"Ariabella Moreau was only the beginning. A proof-of-con-cept, if you will. The modifications she has survived have pro-vided us valuable information, and will enable us to perform these changes upon other pre-adjustment ruanir. Indeed, we have already started. And it is that for which we require your assistance."

Two enforcers stepped from the shadows. They might as well have materialized from nothing.

Alarm shot through me. "Sir?"

"We are affording you a tremendous honor, Mister Marseilles. A unique enhancement to your already consider-able talents."

I looked around fast, searching for an exit. A diversion. Anything. They couldn't do this. Not to *me*.

The enforcers grabbed my arms, pinning me in place. I yanked at their grasp, despite knowing it was useless.

But they couldn't *do* this.

"Don't concern yourself too much, Mister Marseilles," the judge assured me. "We do not intend to waste your mind and your talents by crafting you into the same kind of strakirin as Miss Moreau has become. Quite the contrary. The Judiciary values your… interesting traits. We would not jeopardize a resource like yourself so recklessly. No, we require a liaison between our strakirin forces and our dehaian allies beneath the sea. A commander, if you will."

I paused in my struggle, looking to the judge. "What?"

"You won't be like them, Mister Marseilles. You will be something new. A creature with the powers, strength, and speed of a strakirin, and the autonomy to discern the best course of action for all our underwater projects—including our offensive against Yvaria and other nations."

My gaze turned to Ari, floating in the tank. She'd taken out enforcers. The toxin that lurked in her skin was so deadly, even the judges steered clear. She'd poisoned the Beast itself, or so I'd overheard the lab attendants claim.

And with that power at my disposal… power even the *judges* feared…

They'd never destroy my mind. They said they wouldn't, but if I really thought about it, I knew they couldn't even if they *did* try. I wasn't like anyone else in this world. I never had been. Which meant…

"What do you say, Mister Marseilles?"

I looked back at the foolish old man dressed like a preacher who didn't realize he was about to be consumed by hellfire. I didn't even have to feign a smile. "Anything for the Judiciary, sir."

The Awakened Fate Series continues in
DEFIANCE.

Join Skye Malone's mailing list to hear about
the newest releases!
www.skyemalone.com/mailinglist

Love the book?
Please leave a review on Goodreads and your favorite book-
related website!

Other titles by Skye Malone
The Awakened Fate Series
The Demon Guardians Series
The Kindling Trilogy

ACKNOWLEDGMENTS

I owe many people a great deal of thanks for their help in the creation of this book.

To my mother, thank you for all your support and encouragement as I worked my way through a very difficult time while finishing this story. You've helped me survive more than I ever imagined facing, and for that I am endlessly grateful. No one could ask for a better mother than you.

To my sister, thank you for being someone I can count on, for being a tremendous support to me, and for being your amazing, insightful, butt-kicking self. You're a gift, plain and simple, and I am so grateful that you're in my life.

To my friend, Robin Augsburg, thank you for being the incredible, strong, kind person that you are. I am so glad to know you. Thank you for beta-reading, for all your support, and for answering my countless last-minute grammar questions.

To JC Lillis, thank you so much for beta-reading and all your excitement for this story. I'm so happy to know you (and I can't wait for your next book!).

To Cat Skinner, thank you for beta-reading and your many helpful and detailed suggestions about the story.

To CJ Obray, thank you for your editing expertise and for your work in getting Memory ready to go.

To the folks in the EPL meetup group, thank you so much for how you've supported and encouraged me, how you've read these books and shared about them, and for welcoming me into your wonderful community.

Last (but definitely *not* least), thank you to everyone who has read the Awakened Fate series, who has left reviews about how much they enjoyed the books, who has told their friends, and who has spread the word about this series. I couldn't do this without you, and I am grateful beyond words for the support you've shown this series. Thank you, thank you, thank you.

About Skye Malone

Skye Malone is a fantasy and paranormal romance author, which means she spends most of her time not-quite-convinced that the magical things she imagines couldn't actually exist.

Born in the Midwest of the United States, she dreams someday of traveling the world – though in the meantime she'll take any story that whisks her off to a place where the fantastic lives inside the everyday. She loves strong and passionate characters, complex villains, and satisfying endings that stay with you long after the book is done. An inveterate writer, she can't go a day without getting her hands on a keyboard, and can usually be found typing away while she listens to all the adventures unfolding in her head.

Connect with Skye Malone

Website: www.skyemalone.com

BookBub: www.bookbub.com/authors/skye-malone

Amazon: www.amazon.com/author/skyemalone

Facebook: www.facebook.com/authorskyemalone

Instagram: www.instagram.com/authorskyemalone